When Pacey closed his eyes, he felt like his body had been shocked. A disturbing flash of images raced through his mind. Dust rising off beaten earth. Horses, rearing up in slow motion, throwing riders off their backs. Men in uniforms, Confederate uniforms. These men were being shot, the bullets raking their bodies, throwing the men to the ground. The soldiers stumbled into each other, screaming, their arms rising up to the sky. Pacey's eyes flashed open. He found he was gripping a chair, and had to sit down. He was shaking, breathing heavily. A fine layer of cold sweat covered his skin. He had no idea what had just happened, but he would consider himself a lucky man if it never happened again. He pressed his head into his hands, trying to calm down. In this position, he didn't hear Elolie come in.

She stood in the doorway of the kitchen for a moment, watching Pacey try to slow his breath. A smile crept across her lips as she said, "The dead speakin' to you now, boy?"

Dawson's Creek

MYSTERIES

BAYOU BLUES

Based on the television series "Dawson's Creek"™
Created by Kevin Williamson
Written by Anna Fricke & Barbara Siebertz

First published 2001 by Pocket Books
a division of Simon & Schuster, Inc.
1230 Avenue of the Americas, New York, NY 10020

This edition published 2001 by Channel 4 Books
an imprint of Pan Macmillan Ltd
20 New Wharf Road, London N1 9RR
Basingstoke and Oxford

Associated companies throughout the world
www.panmacmillan.com

ISBN 0 7522 6169 X

9 8 7 6 5 4 3 2 1

A CIP catalogue record for this book is available from
the British Library.

Printed and bound in Great Britain by Mackays of Chatham plc

For Mom and Deb, who had the guts to take me to New Orleans—A.F.

For my parents, all of them, with much love —B.S.

1

Cities of the Dead

Jack McPhee hated cemeteries.

For as long as he could remember, he'd avoided them. They remained the location of horror movies, where vampires and zombies rose from the dead, and the occult came to worship. He knew his fear of cemeteries wasn't rational, but blamed this on his sister, Andie. Andie loved horror movies as much as their friend Dawson Leery, and had spent most of their childhood terrorizing him with "true" tales of ghosts and goblins, and everything that lurked in the night. For her it was a morbid sense of curiosity that drove her to read and watch everything about the subject that she could get her hands on. Because of this, Jack had spent more times than he'd like to remember watching movies he'd never have chosen for himself, feeding a fear that only seemed to grow larger and more irrational as the years went by. Once he tried to discuss it with his father, but was told that he was a man and men weren't scared by things that didn't exist.

He tried to remember this as he stared out the car window at the large cemetery in front of him. Its gates still brought back a fear that he couldn't control. The white fog that still hung in the air didn't help the matter any. Neither did the strange shadows that seemed to dance around the first crypt that stood just beyond the cemetery gate. Whether these shadows were cast by the fog or something unknown, Jack wasn't sure. The only thing he was sure of was that he was alone. Why he'd decided to stay in the Leery SUV while his sister and friends went exploring didn't seem as intelligent a choice as he'd first thought.

Only thirty minutes earlier Jack had sat in the far back of the car, watching Dawson drive, while Andie played tour guide to their motley crew. . . .

"Okay, I've got two votes for the swamp tour, three for the French Quarter, one for the steamboat brunch, one for Jazzland—wait a second. Can't we all agree on one thing? I thought the whole point of going on vacation together was so we'd spend time together."

"When have we ever agreed on anything?" Joey Potter wanted to know. She sat in the backseat, pushing at Pacey Witter's leg, which was inching into her personal space. When he didn't move it, she kicked it.

"Ow. What was that for?"

Joey glared at his offending limb.

Jen Lindley, who sat on the other side of Pacey, laughed. She'd had a feeling that a two-day road trip down to New Orleans would eventually wear a little thin. After all, they'd never been in such a confined space for so many hours. She watched Pacey squirm, not knowing what to do with his legs. Sitting in the middle when you were tall had to be a challenge, Jen thought. She, of course, had never had that problem herself.

It had been only 7:30 A.M., when they reached the outer limits of the city. Dawson knew it was too early to knock on Jen's cousin's door, no matter how polite the invite to spend time on her plantation had been. "Come on, guys, pick a place. We should probably take in at least one sight today, since we're only here for four days."

"I've got an idea," Andie said. She fanned out a group of brochures facedown like a deck of cards, so they couldn't see what the brochure promised. "So what'll it be—pirates and treasure, Civil War saga, the world's greatest jazz and blues, or something else?"

Since Jen had arranged the whole vacation they made her pick, which she did reluctantly. To have her five friends hate the location she drew at random seemed a little harsh to her. As she slowly turned over the brochure to look at it, she was pleasantly surprised. On the cover it read:

Cities of the Dead—Voted #1 attraction in all of New Orleans.

Beautiful aboveground tombs keep the dead dry, forming small concrete cities within the Big Easy. These cemeteries have been nicknamed the Cities of the Dead, the oldest being St. Louis No. 1, 2, and 3, located near the French Quarter. Here you can explore the graves of pirates, madams, and voodoo queens.

As you walk around, make sure to bring some hoodoo money to leave with the original voodoo queen, Marie Laveau, and maybe she'll grant your wish.

The lettering was featured over pictures of eerily beautiful tombstones in mossy gardens, many candlelit, giving them a magical, ghostly quality.

Jen opened the brochure to read more. The pictures inside were even more intriguing. Full of fog and shadow. Angels and saints mounting the tombs, giving a sense that the city was actually populated.

All bodies in New Orleans are buried aboveground because of the city's high water table. When New Orleans was first settled, the people realized that as graves were dug they'd fill with water. The coffins were weighted down with rocks, but after a rainstorm they would inevitably break through the moist soil that covered them, the lids often falling open to expose the now ripe bodies to the sun.

Pacey, who was reading over Jen's shoulder, smiled. *This could be really fun,* he thought. Joey was so easy to scare, and doing Dawson's horror movie a few years back had taught Pacey how to press her buttons. He wasn't going to let this opportunity pass. "So we're all in, right?"

"I'm in," Dawson said.

"Me, too," Jen said.

"I'm always up for anything spooky," Andie confessed.

And then it was quiet.

"Joe, you're in, right?" Dawson asked.

Pacey nudged her then. "Potter, why don't you just admit you're chicken to go?"

Joey scoffed, wondering what she had to be afraid of. *Some creepy old cemetery right out of a bad episode of* Scooby Doo? *Don't think so.* Though she hadn't been crazy about this vacation from the outset, Dawson had convinced her that New Orleans would offer them adventure, which was sorely lacking in Capeside, not to mention the opportunity to actually experience a formal Southern masquerade ball. Not that Joey cared about dances, but the way Jen had described the Percy Ball made it sound like something out of a period novel. An added perk was that their accommodations were free. They were actually staying at the Percy Plantation, which was owned by Jen's cousin, Monique.

Joey suddenly noticed Dawson's eyes in the rearview mirror. She could tell he really wanted to go. "Fine," she said, "but note that I'm going under protest."

"Okay, that settles it. Cities of the Dead, here we

come." Pacey couldn't wait to get there, knowing it was just ahead.

"Hold on a minute, we're forgetting someone." Andie looked all the way to the back. Everyone followed her gaze to Jack.

"Jack, my man, what's your vote?" Pacey pretended to hold up a score card and imaginary pen to tally.

Jack looked out at them and realized he was either going to have to admit his fear, or make up some sort of excuse. "I think I should stay with the car. We've got a lot of stuff in here, and I read somewhere in there about a lot of theft around that place."

"Are you serious?" Pacey wanted to know.

"Come on, Jack. Dawson'll set the alarm," Jen coaxed him.

"I know what this is about," Andie said. "I can't believe you're still afraid of cemeteries."

"You're scared? And I thought it was going to be fun to push Potter's buttons—Ow." Pacey rubbed his leg. Joey had kicked him again.

"You are such a troublemaker. Look, if he doesn't want to go he shouldn't have to. And if you do anything in there to try to scare me, I'll make sure you regret it for the rest of this trip." Joey's eyes said everything. She meant business and Pacey knew it.

"Fine, but this isn't going to be as much fun as I thought," Pacey lamented.

Dawson found a place to park just outside the cemetery. Jen was the first to get out to stretch, followed by Pacey, who put his feet down carefully. His left leg felt like pins and needles as he stomped on it, trying to wake it. Everyone else piled out then—all but Jack.

"You sure you don't want to come?" Jen asked. "I'll protect you." She smiled at him impishly, but it wasn't enough to make him want to go.

Dawson leaned back then and handed Jack his DVD player. "In case you get bored. There are some movies in the red gym bag." He smiled at him and handed him the keys to the car.

Jack watched them as they entered the cemetery, Pacey helping Andie open the huge, vine-covered wrought-iron gate. He could hear the gate creak from inside the car. The fog was so thick he could barely see the gang wave at him as they disappeared into the concrete city.

As soon as they were out of sight, Jack pushed the automatic door lock button. Click. They all snapped shut. He was safe. Then he went for the red gym bag. He needed something to take his mind off the gate in front of him. He unzipped the bag and found a small assortment of DVDs: *The Exorcist, Interview With a Vampire, Angel Heart, Scream, Poltergeist*. What happened to the Spielberg-loving Dawson that Jack counted on? He continued to sort through the DVDs: *The Shining, Jaws*—at least Spielberg—*Jurassic Park*, and finally *E.T. E.T.* it is. Jack put in the disc, happy to see the little brown guy with the glowing heart.

At 8:15, the wind picked up and leaves began to dance across the car windows. Their scraping distracted Jack, who finally looked out at the cemetery again. The fog was thicker now, and Jack wondered how his friends were doing. A beeping noise started to fill the car, and Jack noticed that the DVD player was out of power. He reluctantly turned it off, then picked up the Cities of the Dead brochure, studying it. The place was huge. *They could be in there for hours,* he thought. Suddenly he had the strange feeling that someone was watching him, though he could see no one out there in the fog. The feeling made his heart beat faster, and his mind race. He didn't want to be alone anymore. He hastily put on a jacket and decided to find his friends.

He walked quickly through the creaking gate, past large mausoleums with saints at their crowns. He looked up at the saints for a second, taking in their expressions. With the fog around them, it seemed to Pacey as if they were in the clouds, waiting for God to let them into the gates of heaven.

He continued down a row of crypts that were shaped like houses, their headstones where the doors should be. Dates and names blurred, but he did notice that there seemed to be more multiple graves with the date of death in the late 1870s.

He reached a large pedestal tomb where the road diverged into three different paths, not knowing which way his friends would have gone. They had more than a half-hour start on him. For the first time he had a chance to think, and was careful to not let his imagination get the best of him. That's when he noticed the dates on the tomb in front of him. Within the pedestal tomb were three bodies. Its occupants were two, three, and four years of age. He read the inscription above it:

> DIED OF YELLOW FEVER
> SELBY, MARY AND MICHELLE.
> MAY GOD BLESS THEIR SOULS.

Then he noticed the tomb beside it. It was the girls' mother. She had died a month later. He'd read in history class about the Black Plague in Europe, and how devastating it had been. Looking back at the graves of the vast numbers of people who had died here in the late 1870s, he realized that yellow fever had been the Black Plague of New Orleans. Whole families had been wiped out for something that now could be treated with a pill. The thought was sobering.

He looked at the three paths again, wondering which one would lead him to his friends. Down the path to the right there were a group of angels on the top of a large crypt, their serene expressions somehow offering comfort to those on the ground. For Jack it was enough of a sign to proceed.

Crosses and altars littered the road he was walking down. Candles left by loved ones illuminated many of the graves. He noticed clover growing at the door of one mausoleum, and wondered if that meant good luck even here. That's when he felt it again. Someone was there. He hoped it was Andie just playing some trick, so he called out, but no one answered.

He began to walk faster and faster, his heart beating at the same rhythm as his fast-moving feet. He could feel the blood pulsating in his neck, which only made him think of tales of vampires.

Now he was running. He looked behind him to see who his attacker could be, but no one was there. He slowed down, knowing his imagination had just gotten the best of him. When he turned back to look at the road in front of him, he stopped short. Directly in his path was a woman. She was beautiful, her skin the color of chocolate. She was dressed oddly though, with a kerchief around her neck that was tied in many knots.

"I'm so sorry. Cemetery has me a bit spooked," he started to say.

She stared at him, her brown eyes taking on an amber glow that sent chills up and down his spine. Something about this woman was cold, lifeless. When she opened her mouth to speak, he didn't like what came out of it.

"Evil will come close to you. And the closer it is to you, the more careful you must be. If your friends are foolish, someone you know will die."

Jack started to back away from the woman. He had no idea what she was talking about and didn't want to know. That's when he noticed that her feet weren't touching the ground; she was floating! She proffered her hand then, and that was enough to make Jack take off as fast as he could. This time he was running at a breakneck speed, just trying to get away. For a brief moment he wondered if he'd fallen asleep in the car and this were all a nightmare, but as he stumbled and scraped his arm across a grave, he knew he was wide awake.

He ran faster, deeper into the City of the Dead, just wanting to escape. After a minute, he looked over his shoulder to see if she was following. That's when he ran into someone. They both went down hard. Jack scrambled, pushing himself to his feet quickly so he could flee again, and then saw who he hit. It was Pacey.

"Man, McPhee. I thought you quit football," Pacey said, just lying on the ground with the wind knocked out of him. Jack offered him a hand and helped him up. Pacey finally saw his face. "What's wrong with you? You look like you saw a ghost."

"I think I did. Where is everyone else?"

"I left them down at the Queen of Voodoo's tomb. Some lady named Marie Laveau. You should see her crypt, covered with flowers and money. She's been credited with a lot of good and evil in this town. I think even a couple zombies." Jack flinched. "Sorry, man. Forgot you aren't into this stuff. Why don't we catch up with everyone else?"

Jack was grateful for Pacey's company as they walked down the path. Pacey noticed that Jack's hands were actually shaking. He asked, "What'd you see?"

They were almost at Marie Laveau's tomb now. Jack could hear Andie giving her Universal Studios tour guide spiel.

"Nothing worth mentioning. And please don't say anything to anyone else. That's all I need is Andie teasing me again. She was merciless when we were kids."

Pacey understood. Though he didn't believe in ghosts and goblins, or anything that couldn't rationally be explained, he could understand how someone could mistake one of the statues in this cemetery as one of the living dead. The only reason he'd run into Jack is because he himself had been fleeing. He'd scared himself when he'd cut across a grave to read a headstone, coming face to face with a man. The man had only been a statue, but it was enough to make him run.

They joined the group in time to hear the last of Andie's spiel, ". . . so whoever wants to make an offering should do it now, and maybe Madame Laveau will grant your wish."

Jack pulled out a quarter from his pocket and laid it on the tomb.

"You're making a wish, Jack? That's not like you," Andie said.

"Hey, there's always a first." He closed his eyes then and made a wish—that everyone he loved would be safe. No sense in taking chances.

"I'm glad you're here, brother o' mine." She took his hand and squeezed it.

"So what'd I miss?" Jack asked.

"Just a lot of dead people," Joey said.

"And plenty more where they came from," Dawson said, indicating the expanse in front of them—aboveground graves as far as the eye could see.

"Anyone for the old adage, you've seen one, you've seen them all? I'm hungry," Jen said.

They all stared at the graves in front of them again that somehow all seemed to merge, then at Jen. She was right. Breakfast sounded great.

2
Percy Plantation

They ate at a quaint outdoor café on the Mississippi River. The fog was now lifting and the day was a bright blue. Jen had ordered grits, nostalgic for many summers spent on the Percy Plantation with good Southern food that her aunt used to say stuck to your bones. As she looked down at her food, it was still hard for her to believe that her Uncle David and Aunt Naomi were dead. They'd died in a car accident over two years ago.

Her cousin Monique, who had just turned eighteen, was in her uncle's charge now. Jen remembered Winston Percy as a sweet old bear. He was tall and kind, and used to bring them presents from exotic locations, since he'd been the buyer for the antiques store the Percys owned in the French Quarter. It was

13

a family business, like the plantation, and the Percy men often shared duties on both. Now all of this fell on Winston's shoulders until Monique was old enough to take over or help with one or the other, or both, Jen thought.

Winston Percy had tracked Jen down through her parents a few weeks ago, calling to invite her to the Annual Percy Masquerade Ball. It was actually the first ball since Monique's parents' passing, and Winston felt that his niece could use the comfort of friends and family at a time like this. Though Jen hadn't seen her cousin since she was twelve, she was excited at the prospect of rekindling their friendship. They had been as close as sisters when they were young. Winston had also asked her to bring her friends along, telling her the more distractions for Monique, the better. Anything to keep her mind off her loss.

Jen looked at her friends around the table, happy that they had been able to come. She knew if anyone could keep Monique's mind off her troubles, it was this group. They'd done wonders for her when she'd first arrived in Capeside.

Just then a huge shadow passed over the table. They all looked up to see a riverboat go by. Joey fell instantly in love with it, imagining what Mark Twain must have seen. Dawson could see the wonder pass over her face, and smiled. This was going to be an amazing vacation. Even Jack, who had been skittish seemed mesmerized by the water. It had a calming effect on him, and he began to wonder if lack of sleep or hunger had made him imagine what had happened to him in the cemetery that morning.

Pancakes, eggs, bacon, waffles, and grits. It all smelled great, Pacey thought. It was nice to sit by the water and eat. He'd always loved that. Eating by the water somehow made everything taste better. He cut into his pancakes and put a huge stack into his mouth, wondering what Andie had in store for them next. She was fidgeting with her guidebook, marking with highlighters and stick-it notes. Her brochure was beginning to look like an open-book test.

"Okay, Louisiana Historical Association Civil War Museum, or Mardi Gras World?" Andie looked at their faces expectantly.

"Civil War Museum?" Dawson offered.

"Civil War Museum," Jack concurred.

"Mardi Gras World." Pacey gave an enthusiastic thumbs-up.

"Mardi Gras World?" Jen offered.

"Can I abstain?" Joey asked.

"No." Andie's brow furrowed. She was beginning to think that they really would have to divide up so everyone could actually see something they wanted to see.

"Andie, how 'bout we do a quick tour of the city by car, scope it out, then go to the plantation and get settled in. That way we'll have a frame of reference before we hit everything tonight or tomorrow. What do you think," Dawson offered.

"If you can get everyone to agree on that, I'm in."

"Me, too," Joey said. Soon everyone was concurring. Dawson smiled at Andie. It was settled.

They quickly canvassed the city, knowing they wanted to take a walking tour of the French Quarter and the Garden District, maybe do a little shopping on Canal Street and Wilkinson Row, take in a few museums and maybe even do a swamp tour. Andie kept track of their list, marking and remarking the preferred sightseeing order as they drove out of the city toward the Percy Plantation. When they were a few miles outside of the city she finally gave up. It had become even more painfully obvious that they were never going to agree on anything.

The drive to the plantation took them across dirt roads, and behind swamps whose banks were littered with alligators the size of Buicks. Pacey pointed at the green beasts, wondering what they ate.

"People stupid enough to get out of their cars," Joey said dryly.

They all laughed, knowing that none of them really wanted to take a closer look. Alligators, as far as any of them were concerned, belonged in a zoo, or as far away from civilization as possible. *Anything with teeth like that deserved to be left in peace,* Pacey thought.

After about forty-five minutes, they reached the outskirts of the Percy Plantation. Jen excitedly pointed out where she and Monique had played as children during those summer visits. "God," she sighed as they drove past a gnarled old oak tree. "We practically lived in that tree one summer. Now it looks like it's almost dead."

Dawson squinted in the sunlight. "Is this where we're going?" he asked.

Everyone followed his gaze to the hilltop. On it sat

what was obviously a huge mansion. From this angle they could only see the top floor, which oddly resembled a face. Its large black shutters were the eyes, and its huge front balcony was the mouth, which was stuck in some sort of twisted smile. If Dawson didn't know better, he'd swear the house was mocking him, beckoning him to enter its gates and never leave. The view was made even more ominous as dirt began rising around the black eyes and large mouth, until the mansion was completely obscured by a sudden windstorm.

"What's going on?" Joey asked, concerned.

Dawson pulled the car over as the dust began to build around them.

"Can anyone see anything?" Jack was getting nervous.

Dawson peered way into the distance. As he looked toward the base of the storm he could finally see the source of the problem. "It's a stampede," he frowned. "Look!"

Horses suddenly appeared, racing toward them at a breakneck speed, trampling everything in sight. Young cotton plants were crushed in seconds. A young girl on horseback brought up the trail behind them, trying to rein them in.

"Oh my God, it's Monique!" Jen cried, throwing open her car door. Pacey quickly grabbed her.

"Jen, wait! They're coming this way. This car is our only protection." He pulled her into him, and slammed the door shut.

Suddenly horses were rushing all around them. It was deafening. The car shook as everyone sat paralyzed, wondering what would happen next.

"She's gonna get herself killed!" Jen yelled to be heard over the stampede. She hated sitting there unable to do anything to help.

As soon as the horses passed, Dawson was the first to jump out of the car. One of the horses had broken off from the herd. Quickly mounting it, Dawon took off after Monique.

"What does he think he's doing?" Joey was worried.

Andie turned to Joey and asked, "Did you know that Dawson could ride?"

Pacey did. He remembered when Mitch Leery took Dawson to a dude ranch after *City Slickers* came out. He was always looking for opportunities to bond with his son. These were things Mitch Leery actually thought of, which always made Pacey painfully aware that his father thought of nothing when he thought of him.

Joey held her hand up to shield her eyes from the sun as she watched Dawson wrangle the wild horses. She was amazed at how well he rode. He looked strong and determined on that horse, riding around the outside, trying to catch up with the herd, and trying to cut through the center to slow them down. Monique was also moving around the outside, trying to reach the lead stallion. She was a few strides ahead of Dawson, ready to leap onto the lead stallion, a beautiful black beast. As she stood on her horse and tried to get in sync with the stallion, she was thrown off stride. She could tell that the stallion was going to bolt to the left soon, so she took a breath and made a leap of faith.

She landed on the black beast, but began to slip off the horse. If she fell, the horses around the stallion would trample her.

Dawson put his heels into his horse, forcing it to go faster, maneuvering into the herd until he was riding neck and neck with the stallion. He knew he had only one chance really, putting out a hand. Monique would have to take his hand and he would pull her back up toward her horse's mane. If the stallion jerked, Monique would fall off the horse and the stampede would continue. If he lost his grip on her during any of this, she could be seriously injured—or worse.

She grabbed hold quickly, knowing what she had to do. As Dawson tried to pull her up, she struggled to inch forward.

Joey, Andie, Jack, Jen, and Pacey stared in awe as they watched the two work in tandem, until Monique was finally secure on the stallion's back, her arms wrapped around his neck. She pulled back on the horse's mane, whispering to him as she did, until he finally slowed. As the horses finally came to a stop, Monique turned to Dawson and thanked him, then asked, "By the way, who are you?"

"Dawson Leery. I'm a friend of your cousin, Jen." Dawson indicated Jen, who was approaching with the rest of the gang. A few field workers could be seen approaching in the distance.

"Monique! Are you okay?" Jen ran toward her cousin, who jumped off her horse to hug her. They shrieked with girlish joy.

"I am so happy you decided to come," Monique told her.

Pacey cleared his ears, then turned to Jack and whispered, "Why do women always use sounds only dogs can appreciate when greeting one another?" Jack stifled a chuckle.

Jen turned to the gang and began introducing them. "I want you to meet my friends. This is Joey Potter, tomboy extraordinaire; Andie McPhee, our very own *Let's Go Guide;* Jack McPhee, her very handsome brother; Pacey Witter, boy in desperate need of salvation; and you've already met Dawson Leery, hero." Dawson jumped off his horse.

"It's really nice meeting y'all. I hope you'll have a good time here at the plantation." Monique went to dust her hands off on her clothing, when she realized that she was covered from head to toe in the stuff. "I must look a fright," she drawled.

She was about as tall as Jen, but her hair was almost black, which contrasted beautifully with her alabaster skin. Her eyes were green, with small brown flecks that seemed to dance in the afternoon sun. As Pacey and Dawson stared at her, "fright" was not a word that entered their minds. Monique Percy was the epitome of a Southern belle.

"Put your tongues back in your heads, boys," Joey whispered to them.

"I don't mean to pry," Jack began, "but do stampedes like this happen very often?"

Monique smiled, but it was the kind of smile that was hiding something. Jack had seen it on Andie many times. "This was a fluke. Nothin' ever happens here. It's always as slow as molasses," Monique added emphatically.

"Miss Monique, are you okay? We saw the dust clouds from the north field." It was one of the hired hands. He was older, in his early seventies.

"I'm fine, Caleb."

"But Miss Monique, I think—"

She quickly cut him off. "I'm fine. Horses got out and trampled a few fields. That's all."

"Are you sure that's all it is?" He obviously thought it was something more.

"I'm sure. Now you and the boys take the rest of the horses back to the stables. I'm going to ride up to the house with my guests. If you could meet me up there I'd appreciate it." Monique stared at Caleb, clearing her throat, hoping he would finally realize there were more people here than just herself.

Caleb finally took them all in, as if seeing them for the first time. "Sure thing, Miss Monique. And I'm sorry if I caused any trouble." He took Monique's horse and quickly mounted it, then motioned to the other field hands, each man taking a horse by its halter. They proceeded to lead the still skittish horses back up the hill. The gang watched them work for a minute.

"He moves fast." Dawson was surprised at how agile Caleb was. He didn't expect it from someone so old.

"And spooks easy. Comes with the territory down here on the bayou," Monique said. "New Orleans has a lot of folklore that can sometimes be quite frustrating."

"What do you mean," Dawson asked.

"Never mind. It's not important. Why don't we get you guys settled up at the carriage house? Then we can catch up. Do you think you can squeeze me into your car?"

"If you don't mind sitting on someone's lap. We've got so much luggage shoved in there, I don't want you to get crushed," Dawson told her.

"That's not a problem for me if it isn't for the person I'm inconveniencing." Monique looked out at them. Pacey had a huge smile on his face. Jen quickly pushed him back.

"Down boy. I'm sure we can squish four girls in the back and you can sit in the front with Dawson," Jen said matter-of-factly. Everyone laughed.

"I'm really glad you're here," Monique said, hugging Jen again.

"Me, too," Jen said, as they started for the car. Everyone else fell into step behind them, except Jack. It took Andie a moment to realize he was still back with the horses.

She yelled, "Come on, slowpoke."

Jack had been dillydallying, taking in the expanse of the damage done by the horses, as he watched the field hands drive the horses back over the hill toward the strange house. He turned and picked up his pace to catch up with everyone. That's when he suddenly heard a crunching noise. He'd obviously stepped on something. As he lifted up his foot he was amazed to see dried flowers wrapped in a little bundle, small bones in the middle of the bunch.

Andie noticed Jack bending over. "Did you find something?" she asked, wondering what was taking him so long.

"Nope. Not a thing," he answered, and pocketed

the bundle, not wanting to share it just yet. Not until he knew what it meant. Maybe he was being paranoid, but he also knew Monique was hiding something, and what if it had to do with what the woman had told him in the cemetery this morning? He was suddenly uneasy again.

3

Off to a Rough Start

Jen squinted up at the house and frowned. She had always remembered the Percy Plantation as a classical Southern mansion, with a gleaming white exterior and a meticulously manicured garden in the front. It wasn't that the home was exactly run-down; a high society family like the Percys, even in hard times, wouldn't let their land go to waste. Still, there was something different, something strange about the place. Whereas the large bay windows had once been polished and opened to the world, now they were covered in a fine film of dust, the shutters closed. Her Aunt Naomi had once kept a variety of potted plants on the expansive porch, giving the mansion a sweet, homey feeling. Now the porch was desolate, a single plant abandoned and wilting in a corner. There was a distinct change from the place she had known as a child. The whole house now seemed eerily silent, and Jen couldn't shake the feeling that the home had taken on an almost palpable sadness.

Dawson and his friends stretched and followed Monique and Caleb's lead. They were about to enter the dwelling when they heard shouting from the other side of the house. They followed the noise to see two men arguing quite seriously in front of the stable. One man was older, stately looking. His full face was red with anger and he shook his fist at the young man standing beside an old Ford. The young man was about their age. He was good-looking, with skin that was rosy from the sun and blond hair tousled over his sweating forehead. He glared at the older man with eyes so piercingly blue that you could see the color of them from a yard away. All in all, the girls in particular couldn't help but notice he looked like the typical American hero . . . aside from the rage behind that glare. He was fuming, obviously working hard to keep his mouth shut as the older man screamed at him. Jen nudged Monique and whispered to her.

"Since when do Tom and your uncle have a problem with each other?" Jen asked.

Monique looked very uncomfortable and glanced at the ground. "Long story," she muttered.

Tom noticed the gang's arrival and stared at Monique for a moment. In fact, he kept staring at her as Monique's uncle raged on.

"I've had my eye on you for months, Tom Griffin! It was only a matter of time. You should be grateful

I'm not taking you to court for letting those horses loose!" The older man stopped to take a breath.

"You can say what you like to me—I know I had nothing to do with those horses. I'm heartily sorry for what happened to your crops, but I was across the plantation when they got out."

"Tom," the man said forebodingly. "You know who I am and you know it's not easy to pull a fast one on me."

"I don't even know what you're talking about," Tom said. His tone indicated this vein of conversation was starting to exhaust him, and that he genuinely didn't know what Winston was referring to.

"Well, let me make it clear for you by listing a few things you're responsible for on this plantation. The horses—"

"Mr. Percy, we've been through this—" Tom interrupted.

"Yes, and I'll let you know when I'm done," Mr. Percy retorted. "As I was saying, since we've downsized, you've been responsible for the horses, helping on the field, and helping Elolie with the house, the ballroom included—"

"I see what you're getting at," Tom attempted to interrupt again.

"Then it won't be difficult for you to understand why the finger points at you," Mr. Percy said. "Why, all the horrible things that have happened on this plantation point to one man. To you. I looked in the stable. I saw not only signs of neglect there that could account for the horses escaping, but also a box of tools. Not the plantation's, but apparently your own. High-beam flashlights, small pickax—"

26

"You're right, Mr. Percy, those are my own, and they have nothing to do with anything—"

"I don't think you're in a position to tell me what they do or do not have to do with. As I said, you know who I am, which means you know I mean business." As the words came out of Mr. Percy's mouth, there was an air of finality to them.

The young man glanced at Monique again, muttering to himself, then yanked open the door to his dusty blue Ford. "Yeah, I know exactly who you are. You're a miser, and you're making the people on this plantation miserable. You'd never in a million years be able to replace Monique's father, Mr. Percy. Never."

Tom looked over at Caleb, the field hand, who'd been trying to blend into the scenery. It looked like Tom wanted some backup, but Caleb wasn't ready to provide it. In fact, the field hand seemed very wary and timid in general.

Winston Percy blinked rapidly as Tom's words hit him. He was obviously shocked that their argument had escalated to this level. He glanced over at Monique and her friends. The kids were silent through this exchange. They felt like scrambling into the car and going back where they came from. Pacey leaned toward Jen and whispered, "So, uh, is this the kindly Uncle Winston?" Jen shot Pacey a "shut up before I kill you" look, but she nodded in the affirmative. She was shocked to see Uncle Winston acting so out of character and having a conflict with anyone, especially Tom Griffin, who had always been like a son to him.

Mr. Percy thought for a moment, watching Tom.

He looked like a tired old man suddenly, Jen noticed, trying to dole out the proper punishment. He walked deliberately over to Tom's car. For a moment, judging from the defeated look on his face, it looked as if he were going to stop Tom from driving away and perhaps even attempt to reason with him. Perhaps he had realized that his words had been too strong. He leaned in close to the boy and sighed. "Tom," he began, "this isn't really the way I like to . . ." but then Winston trailed off as he noticed something. "What's that around your neck, Tom?" he demanded.

Tom's hands went to his throat, clutching at his shirt. "None of your business, Winston!" he spat.

But Uncle Winston leaned in and grabbed his collar, revealing a woman's old-fashioned locket. Mr. Percy looked horrified.

"Take that off at once," he gasped. "This is the last straw, Tom. Not to mention the fact it's pretty brazen for you to be wearing that around your neck!"

Tom stammered, uncertain what to say. Trembling, he removed the chain.

Monique broke away from Jen and the others and walked toward Uncle Winston. "I'm sure there's a logical explanation, Uncle Winston."

Uncle Winston turned toward her, shocked. "Really, Monique? Everything seems to point toward the contrary. At this point, logic is not in this young man's corner. That was Isabella Percy's locket," Uncle Winston said. "Of all the things to steal!" He snatched the locket from Tom. Monique immediately stepped forward and took the locket from her uncle.

"I just meant that he could have found it somewhere. Things get misplaced here all the time," Monique said. The tone in her voice was obviously defeated.

Tom shook his head. "Don't bother, Monique. Your uncle's been set against me for months. Though I can't say why. Just goes to show how a man's loyalty can turn on a dime." Tom started up his car, the engine roaring.

Mr. Percy let Tom's words settle for a moment. Then he spoke. "I never want to see you on this plantation again, boy. And on the occasion that I do see you, you and your family will have to pay. Because I will not tolerate vandals, and I will not tolerate crooks, and least of all will I tolerate insolent young men who bite the hand that feeds them." Though his words were stern, Uncle Winston trembled as he said them. In fact, it didn't even seem as if he wanted to say them. But the sight of the locket had obviously made Winston turn a corner. In addition, Tom's harsh words had clearly cut through him. Winston kept his head lowered and walked away, too upset to look directly into anyone's face.

Tom shook his head as the man walked away and shouted, "There's one place you're wrong, sir. I would never do anything to hurt this plantation!"

But Uncle Winston gave no indication that he heard Tom as he disappeared around the side of the house. The look on Tom's face suggested that perhaps he regretted a bit of his hotheaded speech. He looked plaintively to Monique.

"Monique," he began. "I'm so sorry you had to see that."

"Well, I'm sorry it has to be that way between you," Monique said. She was guarded, and formal.

"I don't know what else I can say," Tom said. "This is all a big misunderstanding. Your uncle is obviously worried about money, right? You and I both know he has no reason not to trust me."

"I know, Tom. I've got to find Uncle Winston, okay? And you should probably go." Monique was uncomfortable as she finished her sentence, avoiding Tom's eyes and grinding the toe of her shoe into the ground.

Tom winced when Monique looked away from him. Over the roar of the old engine, he murmured "Sorry," one last time. And then, in a swirl of dust, he was gone.

Monique flushed as she saw Jen and her friends cowering by the wall. She walked over to Jen.

"Oh, Jen, I'm so sorry that the first time we've seen each other in so long had to be under such nasty circumstances," Monique said. "And now your friends are going to think my uncle's some sort of ogre."

"Not at all," Dawson said, comforting Monique. "I'm sorry that we seem to have arrived at a bad time, but we want you to know that we're very grateful and excited to be here."

"And we're glad to have you. That whole thing back there . . . that young man was Tom Griffin. Jen, you know him. I guess he's my uncle's ex-stable boy." Monique frowned, remembering the incident.

"What happened with Tom?" Jen asked. "I thought he was practically part of the family." Tom was their age, and had just arrived at the plantation

30

with his father to run the stables. There wasn't a bad bone in his body. She couldn't believe that he had grown up to steal from this family.

"Well, he was," Monique replied. "I don't really know what happened with him and Uncle Winston. Things have been . . . different around here since my parents died. The entire plantation has gotten out of control."

"What do you mean, Monique?" Jack asked. He shifted nervously, looking around the group. He was starting to wonder why the Percys were being so elusive. What was there to hide? It obviously wasn't a good time to be visiting.

"Oh, it's too complicated to get into," Monique said. "It's just that this missing locket . . . the trampling of the cotton crops . . . They're merely two in a long string of strange events."

"Well, is it strange events, or is it financial trouble?" Jen asked.

Throughout this exchange, Jen had noticed that Monique was becoming increasingly upset. She kept glancing at the clouds of dust Tom Griffin had left in his angry departure. When she had said "a long string of strange events," Jen had put her hand on her cousin's shoulder in comfort. But Monique shrugged her off, wiping away what Jen thought was a tear, and suddenly broke away from the rest of the group.

"I should go find Uncle Winston," Monique said over her shoulder as she walked away.

Jen looked at her friends. Monique had seemed fine when they arrived, even in the face of the horse debacle. "Do you think she's okay?"

Dawson shrugged. "You'd know better than us, obviously, but I'd say not."

The quiet Caleb cleared his throat and spoke gruffly. "Miss Monique hasn't been good in quite a while."

Jen frowned. "What's going on, Caleb?"

Caleb shook his head slowly. "A long story, Jennifer. Too much to hear when you've been driving for two days." He obviously wanted to change the subject. "Listen, I'm going to show y'all to the carriage house. I'm sure you're exhausted, and I should get you settled in . . ."

Jen nodded quickly, wanting to save the man the trouble of getting her friends settled in. "Don't say another word. I'll give everyone the grand tour myself."

"I'll get the luggage," Caleb insisted. Though, in reality, the man didn't seem able to take more than a couple of bags. Dawson didn't even want to let him take that much.

The gang started to walk slowly with the rest of their luggage, following Caleb. Jen felt herself about to ask a question she wasn't sure she wanted to know the answer to. She paused for a moment and looked into Caleb's face.

"So, Caleb . . . what exactly am I missing in the big picture here?"

A shadow passed over Caleb's face, and there was a long moment of silence. He looked from Jen's face to everyone else's; they were expectant. "You have to remember that Monique has been through a great deal," he explained.

"Of course," Jen said. But she knew there was more.

Caleb, however, didn't reveal any more. Instead, he averted his eyes from Jen, and kept the group moving. He seemed to shake a little when he walked. It was the same thing Dawson had noticed with the bags; it wasn't that the man seemed weak. It was more that he seemed nervous. He moved lightly, tentatively, as if ready to take flight. After a moment he said, "The girl hasn't been the same since her parents died, and rightfully so. Still, I wouldn't let her scare you with talk about what's been happening about the plantation. Sometimes it's easier to think something's at work, old souls at battle, instead of just logical explanations. Yes, it's better to just . . . it's just better to think of something logical. Don't let your imaginations run wild like those horses."

The man's words might have been sensible, but he stopped walking and stared at the ground for a moment, as if he were trying to believe himself. Then he snapped himself out of his brief reverie and attempted to grin at the gang, his whiskers stretching over his cheeks.

"Okay, the carriage house is right down that stone walkway. I'm going to go find Monique and her uncle. See if there's anything I can do. You all make yourself at home, and we'll catch up later."

As Caleb walked away, Jack reached into his pocket and found the bundle of dried flowers and bones. He figured now was a better time than any to ask someone who might know about it. He followed Caleb around the corner.

"Hey, Caleb," Jack touched his shoulder. "I'm sorry to bother you. I was just wondering if you might know what this is."

Caleb glanced down at the dried flowers wrapped around the small, yellowed bones in Jack's outstretched palm. The old man's face immediately darkened.

"It's what's called a gris-gris," Caleb said quickly. "Voodoo charm. It casts spells, sometimes for good, sometimes for evil. Where did you find it?"

Suddenly Jack felt that he was giving away too much information. He didn't even know this guy. Jack shifted from foot to foot, suddenly nervous.

"I don't remember. Just . . . around. When we got out of the car."

"Give it to me," the field hand said, panicked. "Those things shouldn't be disturbed—I'll just put it back where you found it. And don't you tell Monique. She's got enough on her mind." Caleb started to walk away again. Jack gazed after the man, watching the gris-gris roll gently in his hand.

Jack walked back to his friends. Jen squinted at him. "What was that all about?"

"I was just making sure we were all set up in the carriage house," Jack said.

Jen looked back at her friends. "Okay, that was weird with Caleb, right?" Jen asked.

"Oh, that was most definitely weird," Pacey affirmed. "Where'd your uncle find him? Some Stephen King novel? I thought he was about to tell me I had the shining."

"I mean, was that avoiding the question or what?" Jen said.

"Not so much avoiding as talking in circles," Andie said. "I mean, what was all that stuff about old souls? All you were asking was what Monique meant."

"Okay, okay, let's not get carried away," Joey said. "I mean, we just came a long way. We've been trapped in a car together. We're bound to be delusional."

"Sure," Dawson smiled mischievously. "Or, you could remember the fact that we're in New Orleans, where anything can happen."

"Thanks, Dawson. No, really, thanks. That makes me feel a lot better," Jack said.

Andie peered up at the house. She wouldn't say it out loud—the timing was bad—but she was excited. There was obviously something going on here, in this house and with this family. She had thought they were just going to experience some Southern gentility, but the series of events that had unfolded since their arrival told her that she and her friends were in for much more.

4

The House That Love Built

The guesthouse was a charmingly furnished, stone-laid carriage house set behind the mansion. The ceilings were high, planked farmhouse style with dark, gorgeous beams of wood. There was a large cathedral glass window on one side of the entry, and a set of French doors on the other. There were two spacious guest rooms, presumably one for girls and one for boys. Each piece of furniture seemed to have been plucked from another era. Jen fingered the tapestries on the bedroom windows; they reminded her of tapestries that would have hung in King Arthur's court. She turned to her friends.

"Isn't this great? God, nothing has changed." She was relieved. So much of the visit had already been jolting. She was glad that this piece of her childhood had remained untouched. Even though when she had visited as a child she had stayed in Monique's bedroom, they had played in this guest-house. They had pretended to be ladies of the court, dressing up in Monique's mother's dresses. The dresses were usually only worn at the masquerade balls, and were intricately beaded, floor-length gowns. The preteen Jennifer and Monique had looked ridiculous parading around in them. Jen got misty at the memory. She suddenly realized just how hard it would be for Monique to experience the masquerade ball without her mother. Aunt Naomi had been renowned for her elegance and gaiety, but beyond that, she had been a warm and generous woman. Jen had often pretended that she was actu-ally her real mother. She hoped that Monique would open up to her. Jen suddenly realized that this was the year Monique would have been coming out as a debutante. Of course—this would have been her coming-out ball! Obviously, she and Uncle Winston had decided not to move forward with those plans. *How sad,* Jen thought, *to be deprived of such a tra-dition.* Monique was growing up so much faster than any girl should have to.

Joey looked around the cottage in awe. Dawson leaned in and whispered, "And these are just the ser-vants' quarters." When she looked at him, he grinned. She was relieved he was trying to put her at ease. After all this time, Dawson still kept her best interests in mind. It was true; she felt a little out of her element in this situation. The feeling wasn't unlike the vibe she got at the Capeside Yacht Club, though she was sure Monique and her uncle were perfectly nice. It was just the idea of coming from money that put her off. She didn't ever think she would find herself surrounded by this kind of wealth, let alone be related to it. Despite her discomfort, she had to admit that the mystery of this house, however seemingly dangerous it might be, was exciting to her.

Jack peered through the window that faced the back of the mansion. He wasn't going to say anything out loud—after all, his friends were teasing him enough about being nervous over voodoo—but he was glad they weren't staying in the main house. He didn't like the vibe he got from that place. Jack gazed up into its shadowy windows. Half of the house looked to be abandoned. No wonder Jen's cousin seemed so sad.

"What say we take you up on that tour of the grand mansion, Jen?" Pacey asked.

"Well, look who's the history student all of a sudden," Joey commented. She was smiling as she said it; obviously, Pacey had done more than enough in his past to stick up for the underdogs in life. Still, she knew he was mischievous at heart and was probably just itching to nose around the house.

Jen stretched and motioned for everyone to follow her back toward the house. "I'm sure it's really different now, and empty," she said as the gang made their way through the quaint, flower-lined walkway. "But I'd love to show you guys around anyway. Maybe Elolie will be inside—can't wait for you to meet her, Pacey."

Pacey perked up. "Ooo—who's Elolie and what makes you think we'll hit it off?"

Jen laughed. "Elolie is Monique's housekeeper, and she's a pretty intense observer of voodoo."

Pacey threw back his head and laughed. "Oh, I see. She's your local tourist attraction and you thought I'd get a kick out of her."

Jen smiled ruefully at her friend. "No, dear Pacey, she is quite the real deal, and I wanted her to meet you because if there's any cure to a troublemaker like you, it's Elolie. She is all business, and she will cut through you in a second."

"Wait a second—why do I need curing? Aren't I lovable despite my antics?" Pacey asked, turning on the charm.

"Sure you are," Jen replied. "I just thought it might be fun to watch you squirm under Elolie's glare. She's got these really intense eyes. Don't even think about pulling a fast one on her, Pace. You'll be dead in the water. I don't even know how old she is, but she seems to have an eternal quality about her."

"Who knows," Andie wondered. "Maybe she's discovered the gift to eternal life through her voodoo practicing."

"Or maybe the water here is really good," Pacey said. "Come on, let's go in. I'm up to the challenge." He personally couldn't wait to get inside and see if this voodoo practicing housekeeper was the real deal. *Voodoo indeed,* he thought.

Everyone got up, following Jen's lead, preparing to take in the looming mansion. Dawson's eyes spanned the size of the house and its surrounding land as they made their way up the walkway. He looked at Jen. "So, new tour guide Lindley, how many people does it take to run a plantation, anyway?"

Jen laughed. "Well, Mr. Leery, such a good question. To tell you the truth, I'm not sure. In the old days, let me see . . . I think traditionally there were six on staff in the kitchen, four maids to clean the house, a butler—man, this is getting ridiculous. And then there were about twelve field hands—I think that's cut in half now. Four men to run the stable and oversee the livestock. And there used to be someone to help with the finances, too."

"Man," Pacey said. "If I lived in a place with that many people walking around, I think I'd want to have some quality alone-time after a while."

"Yeah," Joey added. "If the B&B had that kind of staff, there'd be no room left for the guests."

"Where are all those employees now?" Dawson asked.

"From what Tom said, I guess when Aunt Naomi and Uncle David passed away, Uncle Winston downsized a little," Jen replied.

"Downsized a lot," Dawson replied. He thought about what it would be like to manage that plantation. From the looks of it, getting through even one of the wings would take up a sizable part of the day.

When they entered the house, Dawson took in a deep breath—he always liked to get a sense of a place, its smell, and its history. There was certainly a lot of history in these halls. The interior of the Percy manse was not nearly as dilapidated as the outside; the marble steps of the large, curving staircase still shone under the chandelier in the foyer. Large, richly colored oil portraits were mounted on the walls. The Percy ancestors were obviously a beautiful, haughty breed. Joey peered at one of the first portraits, by the landing of the stairs. It was a portrait of a young, striking brunette with wide, dark eyes.

"This looks just like Monique. Is it her?" Joey asked.

"No, that's actually great, great . . . hmm, I don't know how many greats, Aunt Isabella Percy. But it does look like Monique." Jen looked over at Jack, who appeared to be nervous. "Jack, what is your problem?"

"Nothing, nothing." Jack said. He paused for a moment. In the portrait Isabella Percy was holding a gris-gris. What did it mean? "I don't know, it's just . . . portraits from a hundred years ago that look just like someone alive today. Sounds like the beginning to a ghost story. Just makes a guy nervous."

Andie smiled at Jack. She liked it when Jack's soft side came out. He was always such a rock, so supportive of her; it was good to know that she could help him, too. "Jack, it's just an old house. That's all. We're gonna have a good time here."

Jack knew they were going to have a good time there. He certainly wasn't blind to the adventure of it all, and he was more than happy to have taken this road trip with his friends. Still, the chain of events that had occurred had left him shaken.

Jen, his close friend, could see this in him. She walked over to Jack, comforting him. "Jack, Andie's right. There's really nothing to be afraid of. I spent many a summer here when I was little, and look at me, I'm fine!" As soon as the words left Jen's mouth, she glanced around the room to see if anyone was laughing. She knew that she had made more than her share of mistakes over her high school career. But she also knew she had grown as a person since she had lived in Capeside, and that the five people with her had been understanding of her. Those were true friends, she realized.

"Jack," Jen continued, "you should take a lesson from your sister here and just get excited about the history of this place. I mean, this really is one of the oldest plantations in New Orleans, and practically the only original one left standing."

"Can we look around?" Pacey asked. He was anxious to move around the place, peek into the nooks and crannies. Maybe all those standardized evaluations had been right after all, he joked to himself. Maybe he was supposed to be pursuing a career in detective work.

"Yeah, of course," Jen said. She frowned, wondering where Monique was. And Uncle Winston seemed to have disappeared as well. She considered for a moment how creepy it was that they were wandering around this gargantuan house by themselves. It kind of reminded Jen of the movie *The Shining*. Every step she and her friends made seemed to echo across the polished floors and into the vaulted ceilings. Would Monique and Uncle Winston even hear them if they screamed? Would they hear Monique if something else happened to her? She had just assured Jack that the house was perfectly safe, but she started to wonder if she were the lady who doth protest too much. After all, the house certainly did seem different. . . .

Dawson caught the look on Jen's face. Little escaped him. Since they had arrived, he had been taking it all in. He saw how worried Jen was about her cousin. He hoped that they would all be able to help her get through whatever she was going through. He knew that Joey felt out of place in this environment, but he also knew that the spirit of the adventure would get to her. She seemed a little sad. He wondered if Monique's story had been echoing too much with her own. He caught Joey's eye as she was looking at an oil painting, and she smiled at him.

Even though Joey couldn't relate to this kind of background, she figured she might as well take advantage of it and take in as much as she could. She was concerned about Jen's cousin. Joey remembered the pain of her own mother's death. At least she hadn't been orphaned . . . not exactly. She shuddered to think what it would be like to lose your parents and then have to spend the rest of your teen years in such a cavernous mansion.

Jen sensed her friends were getting bogged down from the earlier events of the day. She didn't want other people worrying about Monique.

"Okay, so come on, let me show you around," Jen said. She took Jack's arm again, smiling. "By the time we're ready to leave New Orleans, we're going to have to drag you away," she said to Jack.

"Oh yeah? What makes you so sure?" Jack asked.

"Because," Jen said, leading everyone into the main ballroom. "Who can remain untouched by the power of a true love story?"

Everyone's jaws literally dropped when they walked into the ballroom. This was not the sort of thing you normally saw in a small New England town. No, this was pure Southern style. To say the room was lavish was an understatement. The vaulted ceiling was painted in the nature of the Sistine Chapel; gorgeous, angelic figures against a striking blue sky. The dance floor itself was polished marble set in a pattern that spiraled inward like a flower.

"God," Andie breathed. "I didn't even think they did things like this anymore."

"They don't," Jen said. "At least not in the rest of the country. But the South tends to keep things pretty old school."

Jack stood in the center of the room, craning his neck and staring at the ceiling. "Um . . . something we should know about, Jen?"

In the center of the ceiling was a huge, gaping hole. Plaster had obviously broken away, revealing the beams in the ceiling and several electrical wires.

Jen frowned. "I have no idea. God, that's where the chandelier used to be, I think. I mean, I assume, judging from where it is. But I don't know what could have possibly happened. It was this beautiful chandelier, too. Multiple tiers, each holding about fifty candles."

"That sounds kind of dangerous, all those candles," Andie said.

"They were more like oil lamps," Jen explained.

"You lit them, then put glass over them." She gazed back up at the ceiling. "I wonder if it fell," she thought out loud. "Something that size . . . it could have killed somebody."

Jen was leading her friends toward a bronze statue centered against the north-facing wall of the ballroom. The statue was of a man, distinguished and attractive in a Confederate soldier's uniform.

"Who's that?" Andie asked.

"That's John Sheridan," Jen explained. "He was Isabella Percy's true love. During the war, he was posted at the plantation to protect the Confederate gold that was hidden here."

"Hey, ho . . . Confederate gold? Hidden here? Well, let's get cracking!" Pacey said, rubbing his hands together. Joey socked him on the arm, rolling her eyes.

"Anyway," Jen continued, "no evidence of the gold was ever found, so we think it might have been a ruse. John and Isabella were lovers before the war started, though. He worked with the mayor before the Yankees invaded, and he was often invited to the Percys' house for entertainment. Even though he wasn't from money, the fact that he worked in government gained him the respect of the Percys."

"So he met Isabella here in her house?" Dawson asked. He was really getting into this story.

Jen nodded. "Yes, apparently it was love at first sight. His first real appearance was at one of the Percys' annual masquerade balls, much like the one we're having this weekend. "

Jen went on to tell them about John and Isabella's

courtship. Isabella's family hadn't wanted her to marry beneath her social standing, but no one had ever been able to deny the charisma John Sheridan possessed, nor the love he obviously had for Isabella. The first night John and Isabella spoke, they had both been behind masks, but John's eyes had locked with Isabella's. She didn't want to speak to or dance with anyone else for the rest of the evening, and from that night forward, after they had danced until dawn on the spiraling marble dance floor, they were inseparable. John and Isabella had planned to marry, but then the Civil War became far worse than anyone originally thought it would. John wanted Isabella to have the storybook wedding she had always dreamed of, and so they decided to wait until after the war to get married.

However, John made certain that he was stationed at Isabella's plantation to protect it. Isabella's father and brothers were fighting the war farther up North, and her mother had fled west for her own safety until the war blew over. Isabella remained, claiming she wouldn't ever abandon the Percy plantation and that she wasn't going to let John die. She put herself in extreme danger as a woman in that town, at that time. The soldiers begged and pleaded with Isabella to leave, but she was determined to stay by John's side. And, in turn, John refused to take safer positions farther north. He was an excellent soldier and was offered various promotions that would have granted him more refuge from the war. But he refused to leave Isabella. Many thought at the time that he had been protecting the gold believed to be hidden on the property, but John's true valor was for Isabella, always.

During a Yankee attack on the house toward the end of the war, many of the Confederates either died or were taken prisoner. No bodies were left behind, so Isabella was never entirely sure what had happened to John.

"Wait, so no one even knew where his body was?" Joey asked.

"No, that's just it," Jen replied. "His whereabouts were always a mystery. People just assumed the worst, though Isabella didn't want to. In a way, that's why their story is so famous here. The Percys always talk about how John Sheridan's soul can never rest in peace, because his body wasn't put to proper rest."

"Ugh, how awful," Andie shuddered.

Jen nodded. "After the war, when the plantation resumed the balls, Isabella always hoped that he would return to her. She looked for his face behind every mask, hoping she would find him like she did the night they fell in love. But she never did, and she died of a broken heart."

Dawson let those last words resonate. He personally thought the story had been amazing. He was always bothered in movies like *Braveheart*, where the main character was fighting a battle for the woman he loved for all eternity, and then he ended up falling in love with someone else. He liked to think that, when there was that sort of intense love in your life, you never moved beyond it, never outgrew it. It touched him that John had not only dedicated himself to stay with Isabella, but also that he had actually stayed to his death. In addition, the fact that Isabella had thrown herself in the face of danger was exciting to Dawson, and moving. This was the sort of passion and adventure he hoped for in his life.

Jen continued out of the ballroom with the others. "Come on, you guys. I wanna show you Isabella's room."

"Isn't that, um, disturbing the dead or something?" Jack asked.

"Yes, actually," Jen admitted. "Which is kind of a big deal in this house, so will you do me a favor and not mention to anyone that we're going up there?"

Jack winced. "Well, if it's such a bad idea, maybe we should—"

"No, no, you're not getting out of this," Jen smiled. "It's just that I don't want you to mention that we're going to Isabella's wing because of Elolie. Saying she's superstitious is a vast understatement, and she makes a big deal about leaving Isabella's wing alone. She only goes in there if she has to, and never, never after dark."

Jack took a moment to think about that as he followed Jen, Pacey, and Andie out of the room. "Yeah," he mumbled to himself. "Let's go exploring in a scary house in a place where no one is allowed. That'll work up my appetite for dinner."

Dawson and Joey remained looking at the statue.

"God, that's an amazing story," Dawson mused. "Talk about true love."

48

"Why, because she erected a statue in his honor?" Joey said.

Dawson looked at Joey, a smile starting at the corners of his mouth. "Did you say that because you meant it or did you say it because you couldn't let this whole vacation go by without some cynicism kicking in?"

Joey smirked, suppressing a grin. Dawson had her down. She couldn't exactly say what bothered her about the story. Maybe it was the whole atmosphere of the house that was throwing her off base. She couldn't relate to this kind of romance and grandeur. In her world, when people left, you knew better than to keep looking for them.

"I mean, I don't mean to insult Jen's family, but it's so easy for us to stand here, decades after the fact, and pontificate on what their romance was like. But Dawson, for all we know, Sheridan died that very night of the Yankee attack. Or worse, maybe he absconded with the money."

Dawson stared at Joey in disbelief. "I cannot believe you are such a cynic."

"Yes you can," Joey replied.

"Okay, yes I can, but why are you getting so ruffled about this love story?" Dawson asked.

"I don't know," Joey shrugged. "Look, I really didn't mean to get worked up about it. I guess I'm just doing that thing where I take you by the shoulders, shake you, and rain on your parade."

"Point taken," Dawson said. "But I for one want to know more about these two. I mean, Joey, come on. How often do we get to be in this kind of atmosphere where you can actually see where these people lived, how they lived?"

"Hmmmm," Joey said. "How about a little place called Waldeck Island?"

Dawson smiled. "Yeah, that was sort of similar. And that was a great experience."

Joey laughed out loud. "Yeah, after the fact." She looked at Dawson for a long moment. "Look, Dawson, don't do this."

"Do what?" he asked.

Joey rolled her eyes, not wanting to explain what she meant, knowing Dawson might be hurt. "Don't turn this whole thing into the movie in your mind. You know, making it more entertaining than it is."

Dawson set his jaw, taking in what Joey said. "Okay, Joe. But, you know, don't do what you do, either." He smiled at her, and he meant his smile as a challenge, and Joey knew it.

"How's that?" she asked, getting a little confrontational.

"You know, setting yourself up to not enjoy something, just because you think it might show you something new. Something you're afraid to experience."

The words hit Joey. They didn't hurt her. They just reminded her that she and Dawson knew each other really well. Well enough to get to the heart of the matter and even hurt that heart a little. She let a beat of silence pass between them, then said. "We better catch up with the others."

She continued following the rest of their friends

out of the room. Dawson remained, looking into the bronze face of the Confederate soldier. He knew that Joey, and even his other friends, thought that he went over the top with his idealism of love at times. And he, if anyone, had good enough reasons to not believe in fate, in soul mates. After all, he'd had his heart broken by his own soul mate more than once. Still, everything that had happened in his life had taught him some sort of lesson. For that reason, Dawson was determined to not become bitter. Besides, what was there to really be bitter about? He was in this amazing house full of history with his five best friends. And as for his true love . . . he couldn't say at the moment what the status was on that, but it wasn't an idea he was about to give up.

Dawson turned away from the statue, suddenly feeling how very alone he was in this gigantic, lavish ballroom. He heard his friends' voices echoing through the hallways, and he shivered for a moment. He didn't know what he believed about ghosts, but there was definitely a presence in this place. He couldn't help but wonder if perhaps Isabella Percy's spirit really did watch over the plantation. Dawson gazed up into the upper balconies of the ballroom, and felt for a moment as if he could actually see where Isabella Percy had stood and watched over the famous masquerade balls, waiting for John Sheridan to return. Joey might play the cynic, Dawson decided, but he knew that when the night of the ball came, she would be swept up in the grandeur. Still, the moment that had just passed between them was obviously a little tense. He wondered how it would play out during the rest of their stay. Sometimes they hurt each other with their honesty. His eye was drawn again to the statue.

Just then, Jen came back in, poking her head around the corner. She looked at Dawson and laughed. "What are you still doing here, staring at that statue?"

Dawson laughed, embarrassed. "I just can't get over that story you told me. I can't believe you didn't mention it before. What an amazing thing to have happened in your own family."

"Yeah, well, you know I'm not much for dressing up the power of love," Jen smiled. "Come on, let's keep moving. I want to check out Isabella's Percy's room, and if we split up as a group I doubt we'll find each other before dinner." Dawson was anxious to see Isabella's room, too. He wanted to hear more about her story. He followed Jen out of the ballroom, their footsteps echoing on the dance floor.

5

Signs of a Broken Heart

Jen walked up the stairs two at a time, knowing that the rest of her friends were waiting. Dawson was right at her heels, anticipating what other details Jen would share to shed more light on John Sheridan and Isabella Percy's love affair. From what she'd said so far, it was a sweeping romance of war that ended in heartache and longing. The mystery of Sheridan's death probably ate at Isabella Percy. Dawson wondered how she'd lived with it.

They were at the top of the stairs now. Jen could see Pacey fidgeting with the handle on a large mahogany door. She'd told him not to open it until she was with him, and knew it was killing him. Pacey had a knack for doing what you told him not to do. She quickly crossed to the door, and thanked everyone for waiting, promising them that what lay ahead was worth it.

The door groaned as Jen pushed against it with all her might, willing it to open. She'd forgotten how heavy the doors were in the mansion, especially the doors in the South Wing, which were rarely used since Isabella Percy's death. Thinking about it, Jen could only remember going into this part of the house once or twice, and only with her cousin, Monique.

As they entered the expansive hallway, Jen remembered why. It was dark except for the small slivers of light peeking through the thick red velvet curtains, which gave everything a ghostly glow. The walls were covered in a dark wood paneling that looked almost black in this light, giving the illusion that the pictures lining the hallway were suspended in midair. Jack, who had thought he'd finally gotten over being scared, felt the hairs standing on the back of his neck.

Andie wandered out a few feet ahead of them and smiled an impish smile before declaring, "This place is totally amazing."

Pacey didn't quite get it. He was standing in the same dark hallway she was and he saw nothing amazing about any of it. "McPhee, are you daft? We're standing in the dark."

"Pacey, what happened to your sense of romance? This is Isabella Percy's private wing."

"If you can tell me what's so romantic about standing in a dark hallway surrounded by dead people, let me know." Pacey was referring to all the portraits of people who had long since died staring out at them from the walls. "Don't these people down here like, you know, pictures of flowers, pastorals, or my favorite, dogs playing poker?"

"Maybe if we shed some light on things . . ." Dawson fumbled for a light switch, coming face to face with an image of a sixty-year-old black woman with a kerchief tied around her neck, eyes amber and aglow. The picture was quite lifelike, so much so that Dawson found himself taking a step back, and quickly asking, "Jen, do you know where the switch is?"

"There isn't one," Jen said matter-of-factly.

"Seriously, Jen. Where's the light switch?" Joey thought Jen was playing around.

"Really, there isn't one. They never put any electricity in this wing. When Isabella Percy died, well, they basically left it exactly as it was."

"Why? Seems really impractical." Dawson couldn't imagine having to bring in lamps or flashlights every time someone stayed in these rooms.

As Jen led them down the hallway, she explained, "It's not impractical when these rooms are off limits. No one has actually stayed in the South Wing since Isabella Percy's death in 1870." She was at the end of the hallway now, her hand on the door to Isabella's suite.

Jack put his hand on Jen's, stopping her from opening the door. "So if no one uses these rooms, and they're off limits, then why are we here?"

"Because sometimes when you break the rules, you're pleasantly surprised," and with that Jen pushed the door open, and went into what appeared to them to be a black hole.

"If you ask me, that doesn't look pleasant," Jack said to the rest of the gang.

"Quit being such a girl," Andie sighed, pushing Jack in. Dawson, Joey, and Pacey followed right behind them.

Inside Isabella Percy's room, they tried to adjust their eyes. What little light that came from the hallway illuminated nothing in this room. Pacey couldn't even see Joey, who he knew was right beside him.

"Jen, is this some sort of gag?" Even Dawson was beginning to doubt Jen. Suddenly a cold gust of wind swept through the room, and the door behind them slammed shut, leaving them even more in the dark, if that were possible.

"No one move, okay?" Jen told them, but she seemed to be far away.

"Where are you?" Joey wanted to know.

Andie, who hadn't been frightened until now, went to grab Jack's hand, scaring the heck out of him. "Not funny," Jack complained.

"I was just making sure you were okay," Andie shot back.

Crash! Something thudded in the dark. Everyone froze for what seemed like an eternity. Finally, they heard Jen say, "I'm okay." And then light came flooding into the room. It was the pale afternoon sun that kissed their faces, shining through the windows that Jen had exposed. She tied up the vibrant chartreuse curtains, a smile on her face. This room was still as beautiful as she'd remembered it. The wallpaper in the room was a green-and-white pinstripe. On one side of the room was a Gothic fireplace, its beautiful cherry wood mantel intricately carved with swirls and flowers. The swirl-and-flower pattern was repeated in the wainscoting that circled the room. The furniture was seventeenth-century French, its centerpiece a beautiful hardwood canopied bed. Even the floor was unique, an interesting parquet pattern surrounding the beautiful blue Oriental carpet that covered most of the floor.

Pacey was the first one to say it. "Color me pleasantly surprised."

Jen announced, "And to think that this room hasn't changed since Isabella Percy's death, except for the chair I just knocked over. It reminds me of those Gothic romance novels that Grams hides under the sofa when I come home."

Andie took it all in, instantly in love with everything she saw, but it was the bed that drew her closer. "Look at this. Isn't that the most beautiful thing you've ever seen?" She sat on the bed without thinking about it, getting a better look at the underside of the canopy. It was covered with a landscape painting depicting a man sitting at the bottom of a hill, three beautiful women surrounding him. From here Andie thought it reminded her of a painting she'd once seen by Claude Lorraine, the foremost landscape painter of the seventeenth century. She'd seen the painting in New York, at the Metropolitan, with her mother. She smiled sadly at the memory, realizing how much she missed her mother. She often thought that if her brother Tim hadn't died, how different her life would have been. Jack's, too.

Jack pulled at Andie. "I don't think you should be sitting on that bed. She might have died on that bed."

"Now that's a morbid thought," Andie said, feeling even sadder.

"Actually, he's right," Jen said. "Elolie told me Isabella Percy died in this room of a broken heart. See the clock on the end table? It was stopped at the exact moment she passed on."

"Twelve o'clock," Dawson said, glancing at the timepiece.

"Midnight. The witching hour. That's why they closed off the wing, knowing that Isabella Percy's spirit would roam the halls. You see, legend has it that on her deathbed she was visited by a voodoo queen. Isabella supposedly paid her a lot of money to secure that she and John Sheridan would be together in the afterlife. The voodoo queen cast a spell that guaranteed this, but the spell was contingent on Sheridan's bones being found and buried with hers. My Aunt Naomi told me that even after Isabella's death, a private detective was kept on the payroll to find Sheridan. Unfortunately, he never found anything, so what happened to John Sheridan is still a mystery, and they say that Isabella Percy still waits for him."

"Voodoo queen? You said there were about five or six greats, so Isabella lived around the same time as Marie Laveau, the voodoo queen we visited this morning. She was supposedly really powerful," Dawson said.

"Yeah, I guess it could be her. I never really thought about it. There's actually a picture of the voodoo queen in the hallway. She and Isabella supposedly became friends before her passing. If she was Marie Laveau, that would explain why Elolie is so careful in this part of the house. She obviously believes in Marie Laveau's spell," Jen said.

"C'mon Jen," said Pacey, "you have to admit that this is just some of that New Orleans voodoo mumbo jumbo that helps perpetuate tourism. I can't believe anyone actually takes this stuff seriously."

"I wouldn't make fun of something you don't understand," Jen warned him.

"Why? Because someone's going to shrink my head or turn me into a zombie? Bring it on. I'm going to say it now, and I'll say it again, there's no such thing as voodoo, just like there's no such thing as UFOs, or leprechauns, or a good school lunch." Pacey was on his soapbox now.

"Voodoo is as real as you and me!" The voice came from behind them, deep and smoky, with a thick Creole accent. It startled all of them.

They turned to see Elolie Gilbou, exactly as Jen described. Her face was weather worn, her hair a mass of dreadlocks. She was dressed in dark clothes, a traditional apron wrapped around her waist. Jen went to hug her. "Cheri, did you knock over that chair?"

"I'm sorry, Elolie." Jen felt bad.

"What are you kids doin' up here anyway? Ghosts don't want no company."

"We'll put it back." Dawson moved toward the chair.

"What's done is done. Now you gonna tell me your names?" Elolie looked at Jen. She had a way of making Jen feel guiltier than Grams ever could. Jen hated this feeling, but knew she couldn't do anything about it, so she chose to move on, and introduced her friends. They all went to shake Elolie's hand in order. When Pacey finally grabbed Elolie's hand she wouldn't let go.

"You really don't believe in voodoo, huh?" She looked at Pacey seriously.

"Well . . ." Pacey thought for a beat, wondering if he should lie, then thought better of it. "No. And do I get my . . . hand . . . back?"

Elolie humphed to herself then, but still didn't let go. Instead she touched Pacey's temple and whispered something low and ominous. Pacey struggled to hear, but didn't understand a word. "Jen?" Pacey was looking for help.

"You should have said yes," Jen said, thinking Pacey really should have lied. Pacey looked at her, wondering what all of this meant.

"You gonna be all right," Elolie said, finally letting go. "Your mind ain't gonna be so closed no more, but aside from dat, you're the same. Now ya'll better get outta here before sometin' bad happens. And I better not catch you in here again." They all stared at her. "I know I don't need to say it twice."

They quickly exited the room, not wanting to upset Monique's voodoo-practicing housekeeper any further. Only Pacey hesitated in the doorway, taking one last look at the woman who he could swear just put a spell on him. What kind of spell he didn't know.

Elolie Gilbou closed the curtains knowing eyes were on her, a wicked smile creeping over her lips. This boy was in for the ride of his life.

6

Omens and Signs

As Pacey closed the door to Isabella Percy's room, he was startled by a cold hand on his shoulder. It was Joey. "Geez, you shouldn't sneak up on a guy."

"She actually got to you, didn't she?"

"Come on, Joe. The only way that woman is going to make me a believer is if she raises the dead."

"Don't tempt fate there, Witter," Jack said. He was standing in front of the voodoo queen's picture, the same picture that had startled Dawson. Except for being older, this was definitely the woman Jack had seen in the cemetery. The thought gave him goose bumps. It also explained the gris-gris in Isabella Percy's portrait. He wondered if he should tell everyone, then thought better of it. Marie Laveau had obviously died long ago. To say he actually saw her in the cemetery sounded crazy, voodoo queen or not.

"You okay, Jack?" Joey asked.

"I'm fine. This place is just . . . weird."

Pacey shook his head. "Tell me about it. It's not every day someone puts a curse on you."

They were about to start down the stairs when Jen stopped short, and turned to them. "Okay guys, I know I promised to show you the rest of the place, but after that run-in with Elolie I think we should find our host." Truth be told, they all thought it was a good idea. Running into Elolie had set everyone a bit on edge.

Knowing that Monique had gone after Uncle Winston to comfort him, Jen decided to try the North Wing first. She opened the door and yelled, but there was no answer, so they started down the stairs, canvassing the remainder of the house, which they also found empty. Dawson then suggested they search the stables. It seemed like a logical destination considering the events of the day, so they headed outside.

The afternoon sun stood in the west like a beacon, illuminating the orchards on a distant hill. *They look like peach trees*, Joey thought. Their fragrant blossoms filled the air with heavenly nectar. She hadn't noticed the orchard when they first arrived, but then she hadn't noticed much beyond Winston Percy firing Tom Griffin.

Jen was a few strides in front of everyone else. She wanted to find Monique quickly. After her run-in with Elolie, she felt guilty for touring the house and not going to her cousin's aid immediately. She obviously needed her. It still struck her as strange that Tom had allowed the horses to escape and stranger that he would actually steal something the Percy family found so valuable. Of course, Jen hadn't seen Tom Griffin in over five years. He was a man now, and who knew what he was capable of?

As they approached the stables they noticed the horses were now secure in a large corral. In a neighboring pen, Caleb was busy replacing a lock on an anchoring post. He told them that this was the reason the horses had gotten loose. "See how the lock is old and worn. I guess Mr. Percy had told Tom to replace it weeks ago. With everything else that's been going on here, I can understand why Tom forgot. Mr. Percy ain't forgivin' him, though." Caleb pointed out into the orchard for emphasis, saying that he'd never seen Mr. Percy so angry, or disappointed.

They followed Caleb's gaze, seeing what he meant. In the middle of the orchard was a large gazebo. Inside the gazebo stood Winston Percy and Monique. Winston was obviously still angry. Tom had been like a son to him, and to betray him in such a way broke the man's heart. His yelling couldn't hide that. And though Monique had set out to comfort him, something had obviously gone wrong. Her body language was defensive. Her arms were folded and she kept her distance from him.

As the gang got closer they noticed the gazebo seemed to operate like a megaphone; they could hear everything that was said.

"I'm not defending him. I just think you're jump-ing to conclusions." Monique was angry.

"Growing up with someone does not designate their loyalty. The evidence is right in front of you, that precious locket you hold. I'm going to call the police," Winston snapped back.

"And tell them what? That someone's cursed our home? That Tom found the locket I lost last week? We've all been frightened by the strange things that have been happening, but putting Tom Griffin in jail isn't going to stop it."

"You're wrong. As much as you and Elolie want to believe in voodoo, there is no such thing as omens or black magic. Really look at the evidence instead of blinding yourself with your heart," Winston told her. Monique considered his words as a Jeep drove up. There was a handsome young man behind the wheel.

"What is he doing here?" she asked her uncle.

"It's time we face facts," he told her.

The man got out of the car. He was tall, and wore a white hat. They were still a couple hundred feet away so Jen squinted, trying to focus on his face, which she recognized. It was Michael Stetcher, Monique's neighbor, and their old childhood friend. Michael was a year older than them, and had always had a huge crush on Monique. For as long as Jen could remember he'd been Monique's shadow, trying to protect her from the world. A gentleman at eight, at nineteen he was truly striking. Jen wondered if his love had finally been requited, or faded away, like an old photograph left out in the sun.

"Mr. Winston, I came as soon as I could. Mo, I'm

sorry to hear about Tom." She hugged him for comfort, which he openly gave her. *They fit together like pieces of a puzzle,* Jen thought. "I have to say I'm still in shock over the information."

"That's not why I called you, Michael," Winston Percy began. "I wanted to know if you could arrange a meeting with your father. I think it's time he and I sat down."

"Uncle Winston, you can't. I'm not doing it. This is the only home I've ever had."

"We're being forced to sell. There are no other choices anymore. The bank is going to foreclose, and I don't want you to end up with nothing, child," Winston countered.

"I'd rather have nothing than watch Stetcher senior turn this place into a shopping outlet. Michael, you know I care about you, but your father's business tactics leave much to be desired."

"Mo, put your personal feelings aside, and be logical for a moment. If you don't sell to him the bank is just going to sell it to whomever anyway and you get nothing. Why not get something?" Michael reasoned.

Monique stared at her uncle but said nothing. Winston Percy knew what she was thinking. "Say it. You think it's my fault."

"You know I don't think it's your fault. It's no one's fault. And if we could find Sheridan's bones—"

"Stop with all this ridiculous talk. The fact of the matter is I didn't get the crops into the south field, so we didn't get our extension from the bank. It's my fault we're in the mess we're in. I failed you."

Monique stared at her uncle, "It's not over yet. We'll find a way," she told him.

"The note is due in a week" Michael said. "How are you possibly going to—"

Monique cut Michael off. "I'll find a way. "

"Mo, you're going to have to be realistic for once." Michael knew how headstrong Monique was and wished she would listen. "My father's making a fair offer. It would be more than enough to ensure you'd never have to work, and that your uncle could retire in peace." She had to know that her only alternative was total ruin.

Monique took Michael's hand then. "I know you're trying to help, but I don't want this kind of help. Do you understand? Now please go."

Michael chuckled to himself at the sheer irony of the situation; he had wanted to help but had only managed to drive a wedge between them. "I can't believe you're going to cut off your nose to spite your face. Fine. Mr. Percy, when she comes to her senses, would you let me know?" And with that he tipped his hat to them and started to leave, running into Jen and the gang, who were now only a few feet from the gazebo. He went to tip his hat to them, when he recognized Jen.

"Jen Lindley, I wish this were under better circumstances, but I'm glad you're here. Please talk to her." And then he left. Monique stared after him.

"Are you okay?" Jen asked.

Monique wasn't sure. Nothing seemed to be going right.

Winston Percy got up then, and put his arm around

Jen. "I'm sure this isn't the vacation you expected, Jennifer. You have my humblest apologies."

Dawson extended a hand. "Mr. Percy, we haven't had a chance to meet yet, but if there's anything we can do to help . . ."

Winston Percy looked out at the young crowd gathered around him and smiled, thanking them all and finally getting a chance to greet them. It'd been a strange afternoon, and he thought that everyone must be hungry and invited them back to the main house for dinner.

"That'd be nice," Dawson said, everyone nodding in agreement.

They headed toward the main house, Monique and Jen lingering behind the rest. Monique obviously needed to talk, but didn't know how. How could she share what she really knew? She didn't want to believe it was Tom Griffin who was behind everything, and what she really thought seemed impossible.

"Talk to me. We've only been here for a little over an hour and Tom's been fired, and you and Michael are fighting. Not to mention whatever financial troubles you're having . . ."

"I don't want to stick you in the middle of this."

"Unless you want us to go home, we *are* in the middle of this. Besides, we're family." Monique wasn't looking at her. "Come on, Mo," Jen pleaded. She knew how private Monique could be. Family secrets were always more guarded when you came from money. The idea was that you had so much farther to fall, but the truth of the matter was that often blue bloods liked to see their own fail. They liked to gloat about it, revel in another's failure. That was probably the impetus for her own family sending her to Capeside, Jen postulated.

Monique finally met her gaze. It was time to tell someone.

"Are you guys coming?" Andie yelled. She was almost at the house and everyone else was already inside.

"We're gonna catch up a bit. Don't hold dinner up for us, okay?" Jen yelled back.

Andie waved back a universal okay, then disappeared into the house. They watched the door slam shut behind her, then looked around. Jen and Monique were finally alone.

"So . . ." Jen waited.

"Do you mind if we go someplace?"

A few moments later, Jen found herself climbing a large oak tree in the middle of the bayou. It was three times as big as the half-dead tree they'd passed on their way in, and held even more memories. They'd built this tree house when they were eleven. She and Monique had run their own kingdom from this high perch, ruling everything on the plantation.

"Do you remember when my dad built this ladder because my mom was scared we'd crack our heads climbing up here?" Monique ran her hand over the smooth wood.

Jen did. Growing serious, she said, "I miss them a lot."

"Me, too. They always thought we'd go to college together. Keep one another out of trouble."

"Too late for that. At least for me. I've had my share, and . . ." Jen found herself crying, not really knowing why. "I'm such an idiot, I came up here to talk about you, and look at me."

"You're the only one who really understands, you know?"

Jen half-smiled, then wiped at her nose. "So tell me. Tell me everything."

Monique didn't look at Jen; instead her face grew serious, scared. "Do you believe in voodoo?"

"Are you serious?" Jen wasn't sure how to react. "We're not talking about small blessings and white magic, are we?"

Monique shook her head. She wished she were.

"All my life I've heard about Isabella Percy and her love for John Sheridan. I never thought about it as a bad thing. Actually, their story always sounded romantic. That is . . . until a month ago. You know about the legend of Isabella Percy and her ties to voodoo. The deal she made so she could be with John Sheridan for eternity—of course, all contingent on finding his bones. They needed to be buried with her so she could be with him in the afterlife."

"I remember. What does this have to do with anything?" Jen asked.

"We found them—his bones."

Jen stared at her, incredulous. "How do you know they're his?"

"Uncle Winston thinks I'm crazy, but it's the only thing that makes any sense. To explain the things that have been happening here. You see, about a month ago, we were plowing up twenty acres on the south side. Caleb hit something with the plow. Something hard. He had to rock the tractor back and forth to get it unstuck. Took him about ten minutes before he did, and continued on, not thinking anything about it. Maybe if he had stopped then nothing would have happened. But he didn't, continuing through the rest of the fields until the sun began to set, like it is now.

"At around seven, he raised the plow and drove back to the barn without ever looking back. When he finally got off the tractor he noticed something stuck in the forks of the rake. It was a human skull.

"Within minutes everyone was there. You see, down here they all believe in voodoo, and when you disturb a grave they believe the dead will curse you until you can give them peace again. No one wanted that on their head, so even though it was now dark, and Caleb couldn't remember on which field he'd had the tractor trouble, so the workers began combing all twenty acres, sifting through hundreds of pounds of dirt, to find only a few more bones. By midnight it became apparent that we wouldn't be able to find this man's entire skeleton in order to put his soul to rest. Fog had begun to roll in and everyone was getting jumpy. Talk of Isabella Percy and Sheridan's bones began to surface. And that's when it happened, that's when I heard someone yell! One of the field hands had found a shrunken head on a stake. As I approached it I heard someone say it looked like me."

The sun disappeared over the horizon then and it suddenly seemed very dark. Jen sat there in shock for a moment, just letting it all sink in. Monique finally looked at her, wondering if she believed her. It was a pretty tall tale, one she wasn't quite sure she believed in herself.

"Do you think someone put a curse on you?" Jen asked.

"No, I think I look like Isabella Percy, and maybe we disturbed the grave of someone she loved quite deeply. . . . So many strange things have been happening. The chandelier that mysteriously fell out of the ceiling in the ballroom, out of the blue. Cows that could be milked the day before now dry as a bone. Voodoo altars found in the strangest of places, and items have come up missing and then later been found next to voodoo dolls. I can't help but think that if we hadn't disturbed Sheridan's bones none of this would have happened. Because now she knows that he can never be with her. Elolie says the evil has come, and is doing white magic all the time now."

"What about Tom? Could Winston be right? Could he be behind all of this?"

"I don't see how, but things don't make sense anymore. If I really thought about it, nothing's made any sense since my parents died. And now I'm going to lose my home to the bank because we couldn't get our new crop in."

Jen squeezed her cousin's hand. "There has to be a way out of this. We'll help you. I promise."

Monique hugged her tight, then asked, "But what about Isabella Percy's curse?"

"I don't know, Mo. I've got to say I'm on the skeptical side, but regardless, we'll get to the bottom of it, okay?" Jen's stomach growled then, loudly enough to make Jen blush and Monique smile.

"Let's get back and get something to eat."

"That's if Pacey hasn't eaten everything."

"Which one is Pacey again?"

"He's the— Which one do you think he is?"

"Well, Jack is the well-coifed one. And Dawson's the blond hero, so that leaves . . ."

"Pacey. Big heart, uses it before he uses his head most of the time. And eats like there's no tomorrow."

They started down the ladder, Jen telling Monique about her friends, pointing out each one's strengths, knowing that they would all offer to help. As soon as she could tell them everything, they would figure out a solution to Monique's financial situation. As for the bones, the more she thought about it, the more she remembered how different things were in New Orleans, and wondered if what Monique said were even possible.

7

Whispers in the Hallway

A while later, Jen and Monique were walking back toward the mansion. Judging from the few lights on in the house, Uncle Winston had already gone to bed. Jen couldn't believe how late it was. She and Monique had taken a long walk to continue catching up with each other. They had walked down the beautiful, tree-lined streets of the homes down the hill from the plantation, chatting with each other, laughing sometimes, and being serious at others. They walked for so long that it almost seemed that they were in another world, away from the problems Monique was facing on her plantation. When they decided to return, the moon was brilliant against the midnight blue sky.

The mansion looked so empty as they stood outside of it. Jen remembered that her aunt and uncle used to stay up late, reading in the sitting room before a fire. Their absence had changed many things in the house, obviously, but the thing Jen was the most conscious of was the silence.

As Jen followed Monique up the walkway, she felt a slight chill. It was the same sort of feeling she had after watching a scary movie; the feeling that someone was watching her, or was walking two steps behind her.

Monique turned around and whispered to Jen. "Sorry, I know it's kind of depressing in here. We don't really keep any lights on anymore because we're trying to cut down on the electric bills. Heating, too. Kinda stupid that we're having a ball, but the only reason we can afford to is that the last kind souls in this town are helping us for free. My room is freezing, even for this time of year. And this time of night . . ." Monique trailed off and sat down on the stairs leading up to the porch.

Jen walked over and sat down beside her. "This time of night what?"

Monique shook her head, smiling slightly in the dark. "Nothing . . . I just don't want you to think I'm crazy."

Jen laughed out loud, her laughter echoing into the high eaves of the house. "Monique, never in a million years would I think you were crazy. You forget who you're dealing with."

"Well, I just didn't know if you'd wanna stick around, because Elolie has been walking around at night, doing voodoo, and I didn't want you to be afraid," Monique said.

Jen thought for a moment about what her cousin was saying. It was true; her first instinct was to shiver at the thought of Elolie wandering around in the dark murmuring her voodoo chants. But then Jen reminded herself that Elolie only practiced white magic.

"I'm not afraid," Jen concluded. "But I am glad you warned me. Does she do that all the time, or only lately?"

"Only lately," Monique explained. "Because of everything that's been happening. She's trying to calm down Isabella's spirit. I've been helping her. I mean, I wouldn't claim to know half as much about voodoo as Elolie does, but I help out where she needs it." Monique paused for a moment, biting her lip. "Do you wanna stay and see what I'm talking about?"

Jen smiled. She remembered her own attempts at witchcraft with Pacey on Witch Island. She never really did know for sure if the spell had worked or if it had just been their hormones at work that night. Still, she couldn't deny the fact that she was curious about such practices.

"Sure." She grinned at her cousin.

The two girls ventured into a small clearing under a dying oak tree. Jen shifted nervously in the dark. "Is this really where the magic happens?"

"Usually I just wait for her," Monique explained to Jen. "She has this whole preparation thing, and she doesn't like being interrupted. Not even by me."

"Preparation?" Jen asked.

"Yeah," Monique replied. "She gathers ingredients

for the spells around the property, and then she performs the ritual over there, under Isabella's window." Monique pointed off to the side of the house, where the windows in Isabella's forbidden wing were dark and abandoned.

"Why doesn't she just go into Isabella's wing, if she wants to put her spirit at peace?" Jen asked.

Monique shot her cousin a look. "You know she doesn't go in there at night, and only in the day to clean. That's just how she feels about it. Besides, she believes that Isabella's spirit is everywhere around this house, not just contained in her wing."

Jen took a moment to breathe in the night air. She heard rustling in the deep woods around them, and wondered if it was Elolie, gathering what she needed in the dark.

"It's so different here," Jen said. "So quiet. Not only because your parents are gone . . . it's like the house has a personality, and it's in mourning."

Monique nodded. "I think that's just how the three of us affect it. The house was even too big for us when Mom and Dad were alive, but they were so . . . happy, you know? Always entertaining. The house was always filled with people and with plans. Now that it's just the three of us here, spread out all over the house, it seems desolate. This place never scared me before, but now . . ."

Jen leaned in, nodding. "I know, Mo! I was telling my friends how excited I was to come here—and this isn't supposed to be in offense to you—but the house has this air now. This feeling of something being around the corner."

"I know," Monique sighed. "I don't know what it is, either. I've talked to Elolie about it. Uncle Winston would just think I was crazy."

"Does Elolie think something's wrong with the house specifically, or is she just practicing voodoo for Isabella?" Jen asked.

"I think the two might go hand in hand. She says she senses something. A presence. A presence of something bad," Monique said.

The two girls stood in silence, allowing the words to sink into the air. Jen had no idea what to say in reply. She didn't doubt her cousin. She knew Elolie, and she knew that Elolie was the real deal. If she sensed something bad around the house, chances were she was right.

"Does she know who's behind the mysterious happenings?" Jen asked.

"No," Monique shook her head. "We all have our speculations, like I told you before, but Elolie is trying to get to the heart of the matter. She says that something keeps blocking her visions. She says maybe it's too close to her for her to be able to truly see it, which is pretty insane to think about. I mean, at this point, Jen, I've thought of everything. Every possibility."

"Like, even ghosts?" Jen asked.

"I know it sounds crazy," Monique replied. "But there's not a logical explanation to any of this, so why bother being logical? Elolie's certainly looking into it. Whatever she's saying in her practice lately . . . it's different from the chants I usually hear. I don't know—I can't claim to understand Elolie's inner workings. I've known her all my life, but it kind of freaks me out, you know?"

"Well, because usually Elolie isn't out fighting evil, she's just doing good," Jen said. Monique nodded.

"That's exactly what she's doing," Monique said. "I asked her one morning, because I thought she was protecting me. She says she is, in a way."

"What about Tom?" Jen asked. "I mean, is Winston right? Is he trying to screw you guys over?"

Monique looked away, and shook her head vigorously. "It's not Tom. You remember Tom from way back, Jen, and you know he wouldn't do that."

"Well, I know," Jen conceded. "Still, it seems like he and your uncle obviously have a rift, and maybe that's why." Jen knew that Monique knew Tom better than she did, and she couldn't help but wonder if there was something more. She didn't think that Uncle Winston would get upset for no reason at all.

"It's not why. I don't think it's a person at all, if you know what I mean," Monique replied, and then she fell silent.

Elolie, with her typical impeccable timing, emerged from an opening in the tangled cypress trees at that very moment. Her face was lit from below with candlelight, casting long shadows below her eyes. She looked even more serious than she usually did, which was a little sobering at that time of night, outside no less. She cast her stern gaze on Jen.

"You, too?" was all she said. Jen nodded, glancing at Monique. She suddenly wondered if she was intruding, but Monique gave her hand a comforting squeeze to convince her otherwise.

Elolie started walking ahead of them, her long white gown swishing in the black velvet night toward the window under Isabella's wing. Jen and Monique walked a few steps behind her. Almost unconsciously, Jen found herself tiptoeing, holding her breath.

Monique leaned in to whisper to Jen. "Just do what I do," she said. "I don't exactly know what I'm doing, but she hates it when you ask questions. She'll give you a powder, and we'll rub it on the stones by the outside of the house. Then she does a chant, but you don't have to follow along because you won't know it. Just think good thoughts—it's what she wants you to do."

Jen nodded, her heart racing. She had never done anything like this. Despite the fact that she felt badly for her cousin and the chaos that reigned over her home, Jen was still excited to be involved.

When they came to the side of the house under the lonely, abandoned wing, Elolie stood there for a moment, and whispered something three times, fast, in a language Jen couldn't recognize. Then she turned around and motioned for Jen and Monique to hold out their hands.

When the girls held out their hands, palms up, Elolie sprinkled each of their hands with a soft, white powder that shimmered in the moonlight. Jen didn't know why, but she instinctively thought that the powder was made from crushed bone. She shook off the chill that the thought gave her, and concentrated on what was happening.

Elolie began to sing in a low, haunting voice. Her

lips barely moved. In fact, you could hardly even tell that the voice was coming from Elolie, as the musical sounds seemed to echo through the gently stirring trees, resonating in Jen's shoes and in her trembling hands. The words were foreign to Jen—perhaps it was Creole—but Monique began to sing along as well, in a soft, melodious voice. Jen just watched them, in awe. Then, Elolie reached into the pocket of her gown, gathering more of the same powder she had given to Jen and Monique. She moved forward, tracing the powder in a shape similar to that of a flower on the thick stone slabs that rested beneath the foundation of the old mansion as she continued to sing. Elolie then turned her head slightly and nodded at Monique. Monique touched Jen's shoulder, and the two of them moved forward and began to use their own powder to trace over the pattern Elolie had made. Monique and Elolie continued to sing, while Jen just took in the drama of the moment.

Suddenly, Elolie stepped away from the house and fell silent. She continued to walk away from the two girls until her white nightgown disappeared into the darkness of the gnarled oak trees.

Monique turned to Jen and put her finger to her lips, indicating that Jen should be silent also as they walked away from the house. When they got back to the porch, Monique let out a breath and smiled at Jen, excited.

"Pretty cool, huh?" Monique said.

Jen nodded. "Yeah, that was. . . . Do you do that every night?"

"Lately we have," Monique nodded. "But she

doesn't always do it with me. And she comes out later, like I said. But I don't know what she's doing then. I think it might be something carried on from Marie Laveau. Old voodoo."

"Wow," Jen breathed. She scanned Monique's face for a moment. Her cousin had grown up so much in the face of all this tragedy. She was learning things that Jen would probably never encounter in her life—anywhere outside of the Percy Plantation.

As Monique stretched and yawned, Jen realized once again how late it was getting. "Well," she said, "as much as I would love to stay here and practice my amateur voodoo through the night, I should probably get back to the guesthouse. At this point, my friends are going to think I've gone off to meet the ghost of John Sheridan."

Monique laughed. "Yeah, right," she said. "Well, I'm really glad you could be here tonight, and I'm sure Elolie was, too. But don't talk about it too much. . . . I'm sure your friends are nice, but I don't want to risk anyone making a joke out of it."

Jen started to tear up as she hugged her cousin. "Monique," she said, "I know we talked about this earlier, but I can't tell you how sorry I am that I dropped off the face of the earth the way I did. It was immature, and I betrayed you. We were so close . . ."

Monique took Jen by the shoulders. "Listen, Jen, two play at that game. I understand what you did—a lot of my friends reacted in the same way, because they didn't know how to deal with death. But I did my part in alienating myself. I totally closed myself off from the world. You probably wouldn't have been able to get hold of me if you tried. Don't worry about it anymore, okay? You're here now."

Jen nodded, and watched as Monique disappeared into the dark mansion, the heavy old door swinging shut behind her. As she stood there alone in the night, Jen suddenly felt nervous again. The tones from Elolie's song still seemed to hang in the air. She was relieved that her relationship with her cousin was still intact. Obviously, they had grown up in many ways, for better or for worse, but they still had the souls of those two little girls who had played in the tree house on the bayou.

Jen's night vision was failing her. She reached her hands tentatively out in front of her in the dark. Her skin had suddenly grown cold.

"Okay," she whispered to herself. "Move, feet."

She started to walk slowly toward the guesthouse. She still couldn't shake the feeling that she was hearing things in the dark. In fact, she felt very much like she heard whispering in the air, though she wondered if it was simply the trees and her mind was playing tricks on her. She had just reached the edge of the walkway when she suddenly realized that she wasn't imagining the whispering at all.

In fact, it was right behind her.

Jen turned around slowly, so as not to draw attention to herself. Elolie was walking slowly behind her in the dark, holding a different, larger candle close to her chest. She seemed to be in a trance, murmuring to herself in a different tone than before. Although Jen realized Elolie wanted to be alone at this time, she whispered her name nevertheless. Elolie didn't respond, however. She merely continued walking, the long shadows cast from the candle looming over her face. Jen wondered why Elolie did this different chant, and why she did it alone. There must be more to keeping Isabella's spirit at peace than Jen knew. It frightened her to see Elolie in this way, especially when she acted as if Jen wasn't even there.

Jen was chilled to the bone, and quickly turned around to flee toward where her friends were. She could barely see two feet in front of her face, but she raced over the cobblestones, eager to get back to her friends in the carriage house, which, for now anyway, was untouched by the darkness that had taken over Percy Plantation.

8

A Light in the Darkness

Joey was exhausted from the events of the day. Everyone else was still in the main room of the guesthouse, but Joey needed a few minutes away from her friends. Arriving in New Orleans had obviously been a taxing event. The trip down had been fairly exhausting, especially when it had been her turn to drive and Dawson and Pacey had joked the whole time about her less than stellar driving skills. Despite the fact that she was pretty sure she could parallel park better than either of them, the fact that she'd learned to drive late in life had never ceased to be amusing for the boys.

Joey ran her hand across the soft down comforter on the bed she was sharing with Jen. Andie would be sleeping on the twin bed beside them, since apparently she kicked when she slept and Jen and Joey had hastily agreed they wanted no part of that. Joey couldn't help noticing that even the guest bed in this little cottage was nicer than her own bed at home, the blue flannel sheets almost as soft as velvet.

Jack and Andie were playfully fighting for the sink in the bathroom as they brushed their teeth. She guessed that Jen was still saying good night to Monique. She had wanted some more alone time with her cousin before she came in to join her friends for the night. Pacey was flipping through one of Andie's guidebooks to New Orleans. He had to admit, it was pretty helpful. He was excited to get out and explore the city tomorrow. He was sure it had something to offer aside from voodoo mumbo jumbo. Pacey didn't want to fall into those tourist traps; he wanted to experience the real deal. He shook his head, still not believing the bizarre encounter he'd had with Elolie. How on earth could a person tell from briefly meeting you that you were close-minded? Besides, he told himself, he was quite the opposite of close-minded. He was always more than willing to experience new things. It's just that the new things he wanted to experience included partying in the French Quarter, not quartering a live chicken.

Dawson ducked his head into the girls' bedroom to say good night to Joey.

"Quite a day, huh?" he said.

Joey looked up, relieved to see Dawson. Sometimes he was the only person she really felt like talking to. She obviously enjoyed being there with everyone, but she had known Dawson the longest, and the best. At the end of a trying day it was sometimes a comfort to be with an old friend, someone you didn't have to explain everything to. "To say the least," she replied.

"You okay?" Dawson asked.

"Yeah, of course I am. I'm just a little beat. Adjusting to the decidedly creepy surroundings," Joey said. She flopped down on the bed, grabbing onto a pillow. Dawson sat down beside her. He had partially come in because he felt a little odd about the conversation he and Joey had had in front of John Sheridan's statue. Though it was one in a long string of heated discussions the two of them had shared, Joey had seemed almost angry and he wanted to check in.

"Hey, so . . . is everything okay with us? Things got a little heated in the ballroom earlier," Dawson said.

Joey laughed and looked at Dawson. "Never in my life did I think I would hear that sentence," she said. " 'Things got heated in the ballroom.' " Dawson laughed with her. It did seem ridiculous. "No, of course everything's fine," Joey said. "I'm surprised that even set you off. You know the typical bitter Potter stance on love and the notion that a true form exists."

Dawson looked at Joey, a twinkle in his eye. There was no way he was going to let her get off that easily. Joey fell back on her old sarcasm time and time again, but she'd had enough happiness in her life to recognize it when she saw it. Sometimes he wondered if she was just bitter for the sake of it.

"Joe, come on," he said. "I think you've had some love in your life."

Joey quickly looked away from Dawson, smiling to cover up the awkward moment. Of course she had, she thought to herself. And more than once . . . but what about all the complications that surrounded that love. She wondered if the pain of the experiences had outweighed the actual experiences. She couldn't look Dawson in the eye—she was afraid her face would show what she was thinking—so she stood up and walked over to the window.

"Well, you're right. I guess I'm not one to talk. Maybe I just feel like someone has to resist being swept into the grandeur of this plantation and the dramatic love story that haunts its grounds." Joey was kidding, but as soon as she looked out the window, she got a chill as she saw the gnarled limbs of the oak tree scratching against her window. Joey chided herself. What was she getting so nervous about? This was Jen's family. Really, when she thought about it, there should be nothing creepier about visiting this plantation than visiting Dawson's Aunt Gwen out in the country.

Except that there was something creepier about this place. As much as she would have liked to leave the spook factor up to Jack to deal with, Joey felt that there was something decidedly spooky about that house. She didn't want to say haunted, but she felt something in the air, a chill that wasn't natural. She looked into its mournful windows, pitch black and gaping in the night, the moon only illuminating spots and odd angles of the house through the overhanging oak trees. She could see no signs of life inside. Monique must have fallen asleep immediately after Jen left, because Joey couldn't even see a light where Monique's window should be. And it seemed that Uncle Winston had gone to bed hours ago. Joey rubbed her eyes. She realized that she should probably just go to bed herself. She was starting to read too much into things, and this was supposed to be a vacation.

Just then, Joey noticed a faint, flickering light in the south wing of the house. She was about to think nothing of it, until she asked herself two questions: *Why would someone be walking around the house with a candle when it was the 21st century? And why on earth was someone on that side of the house?* She remembered that it was the South Wing of the house that had been Isabella Percy's quarters. No one was allowed . . . except for Elolie, Joey remembered with a sigh of relief. Surely that was an explanation. But no . . . Jen's words echoed in her head as if it were being replayed in a movie. Elolie did everything she could to stay out of Isabella's wing. She didn't go in there. *And never, never after dark.* After experiencing the dark and looming wing herself, Joey couldn't imagine why anyone would want to go there after dark at all. Those rooms had seemed haunted in broad daylight . . . if you believed in such a thing. Joey gasped. The light came closer to the window, almost illuminating a figure.

"Dawson!" she said, but for some reason she whispered, panicked. Dawson came up behind Joey, holding onto her shoulders.

"What? What is it?" he asked urgently.

However, when Joey pointed to where she had seen the light, there was nothing there. The wing looked as dark and abandoned as before. Joey turned around to face Dawson.

"Dawson, there was something there," she insisted.

"What kind of something?" Dawson asked.

"A light," Joey said.

Dawson took a moment. He didn't want Joey to think he doubted her, particularly when he was trying to ease her away from being so skeptical in the first place. Still, he couldn't imagine why anyone would be in that part of the house. It was clearly closed off, a rule it was obvious that everyone in the household took seriously.

"Maybe it was just a reflection, Joe. You know, of the lights that are on in here."

Joey cocked her brow at Dawson. Was he kidding? She wasn't an idiot. She knew how the laws of physics worked and knew what was a reflection and what was real. This had definitely been real. And he knew as well as she did that it wasn't Elolie; they had both gotten the impression that she was not a woman who took her vows and habits lightly. But Joey was tired, and maybe she had her directions mixed up. Maybe it hadn't been the South Wing, after all. Joey sighed, letting out a huge breath. She was determined not to let this affect her, not in front of Dawson. She turned around and walked back toward the bed.

"I guess it's just time for me to go to sleep," Joey said, attempting a smile. "Enough for one day, right?"

"Right," Dawson smiled. "You sure you're okay?"

"Positive," Joey replied. She walked over to the bed and turned down the covers. "See ya in the morning, Dawson."

"Okay, Joe, sleep well." Dawson turned to walk back into the main room when suddenly Joey released a blood-curdling scream! Dawson whipped around to find Joey backed up against the wall, pointing at the bed.

Where Joey had pulled the sheets down, a long, bright green snake was darting and weaving across the sheets. "Get it off, get it off!" Joey yelled.

Upon hearing Joey scream, Pacey, Andie, and Jack had rushed in from the main room. "Joe, what's wrong?" Pacey asked. He spotted the snake. "Well, that's not exactly a welcome bedfellow."

"I am so not sleeping in that bed tonight," Joey said.

"You guys, you guys, it's okay. It's just a garden snake, it's totally harmless," Dawson said.

"Oh, okay, thanks Crocodile Hunter. As much as I'd like to go on and hear the mating ritual and ancestry patterns of this particular species, can we please remove it from my bed?" Joey pleaded.

"Well, well, look at the tough girl," Pacey smiled. "I'll get a box." Pacey ducked into the next room.

"I am a tough girl," Joey called after him. "I choose to not touch snakes. That is me being tough."

"Joe, you know I'm kidding!" Pacey said as he came back in with a cardboard box. He motioned to Dawson and Dawson leaned forward slowly to reach for the snake.

"Hey, just curious . . ." Dawson said quietly, trying not to scare the snake. "But how did this turn into a guy thing?"

"It didn't," Andie replied. "You'll notice Jack isn't helping."

Jack looked at his sister in shock. "Well, no! I mean, how many people do they need to help them?"

"Mmm-hmmm." Andie said.

"I am not scared of snakes," Jack insisted. "I'm just secure enough with my masculinity that I don't feel the need to tamper with nature's process."

Andie laughed and knocked Jack on the shoulder. Dawson successfully snatched the snake and eased it into the box Pacey was holding. Joey winced as the snake wriggled in Dawson's hand. Pacey quickly went outside to let the snake loose.

Just as Pacey released the small snake into the night, he heard another blood-curdling scream from the darkness. Jen Lindley emerged from the general area in which he'd tossed the snake.

"Hello! City girl here! Please refrain from throwing out small reptiles on my feet!" Jen cried.

"I'm sorry, I'm sorry. Why are you lurking there in the dark, anyway?" Pacey asked.

"I'm not lurking—I'm just coming back from talking with Monique," Jen explained. "Um . . . sorry, this just occurred to me, but why are you coming from inside the house with a snake to begin with?"

Pacey shook his head and led Jen back inside the house, explaining that the snake had been in the bed she and Joey were sharing. Jen's face paled when

Pacey told her, and they walked into the bedroom where the others were gathered.

The six friends stood around the bed and were quiet for a moment. Joey finally spoke up.

"Things like that don't . . . happen naturally," she said.

"No, no they don't," Andie said.

"You guys, these houses are old. Maybe there was a crevice in the wall somewhere . . ." Jen trailed off, realizing that she didn't really have solid ground to stand on.

"But how on earth would a snake end up in their bed?" Jack asked. "It doesn't make any sense." He knew that everyone thought he was being a chicken, and maybe, initially, he had been. He couldn't help it—the whole air of the plantation and New Orleans in general had given him the creeps. But he had gradually settled into his surroundings, and he was sure of it now; he wasn't making this stuff up. Something was going on. He didn't think it was a good idea that Pacey was messing with Elolie, the voodoo housekeeper. In fact, he thought it would be pretty smart for all of them to sleep with one eye open.

"I don't know," Dawson said. He shook his head. He wondered how long the snake had been there. The whole time he and Joey had been talking? While they had been sitting on the bed together?

"You know what? I'm not saying this to offend anybody, but I gotta say that I'm with Jack, here." Joey admitted. She turned to Dawson. "New Orleans is not the charming picture you painted, Dawson."

"Well, Joe, I didn't put a snake in your bed," Dawson defended himself.

"No, of course you didn't," Joey said. "I know that. It's just . . . you have to admit that a lot of sketchy things have happened since we arrived."

Jack nodded. "You guys know that I'm not always this jumpy. I mean, I know we've been joking about it . . . I'm really not trying to make a deal out of things at all. I know we all came here to have a good time, but certain signs . . . Okay, like even the simple fact that the portrait I saw on the wall was the same woman I saw in the cemetery! Doesn't that freak anyone out?"

"They're not signs," Pacey insisted. "Don't let that voodoo woman from the graveyard freak you out. That's what started this, right? Man, that woman is probably paid by the tourist society to wait on the edge of town for unassuming youngsters. Nothing evil is here, we just . . . happened to arrive on the worst day possible."

His words sank into the room. The moment he spoke them, even Pacey realized he wasn't convinced by his own reasoning. If today was the worst day possible, what did the rest of their vacation hold? They had clearly come at a time that was very stressful for Monique and her uncle.

"Well, Pace, it's really not all a hoax. I mean, this is kinda new to me, too, but it's a fact that Isabella struck a deal with Marie Laveau, a deal that said she would be reunited with John, no matter what. Who knows if there are ghosts in the world? I don't know. But if anyone could make herself appear again in the afterlife, I wouldn't be surprised if it were Marie

Laveau. She's not just a fantastical figure made up for tourist traps. She was the real deal—I mean, it's recorded in my own family history."

"So, what are you saying?" Joey asked. "That Isabella and Marie Laveau are still in cahoots to make something happen?"

"I'm saying it doesn't seem as entirely unlikely as it once would have," Jen said.

Pacey nodded, sobered by Jen's words. Then he and Jack started walking around checking the locks on the doors and windows. Jen cleared her throat and looked at Joey, Andie and Dawson. "You guys . . . I certainly didn't mean for the trip to be like this. I know we're walking into a minefield and I don't really know what to tell you." Jack walked back in and rubbed his hand on Jen's back. "Hey, that's so not your problem. Don't worry about us."

"Yeah," Pacey agreed. "At the very least, this is an adventure. If something sketchy starts happening, we've just got to stick together. We've got nothing to be afraid of."

Jen glanced at Joey. She knew that Joey had been shaken up. She couldn't exactly figure out what was bothering her. She knew that Joey and Dawson had had a brief moment in the ballroom and she wondered if maybe it had led to a deeper problem.

"You okay, Joey?" Jen asked.

"Yeah, I am, Jen. I'm sorry. It's just . . . well, not the best thing to happen on not the most normal of days."

Jen nodded. "I totally agree. Let's just pull back the sheets and make sure there's nothing else waiting to greet us in the night."

Dawson helped the girls shake out the sheets and remake the bed. When it was clear that there was nothing else lurking beneath the linens, Jen sat down on the edge of the bed for a moment.

"Will you guys do me a favor?" Jen asked.

"Of course," Dawson said.

"Just please don't mention this around Monique, okay? I know that this was just a harmless garden snake, but I don't want her mind working about how a snake got into your bed. Know what I mean? I think there are already too many things on her mind and this would only push her over the edge. It's a little weird around here after hours, you know? Elolie's walking around with candles . . . it's enough to make anyone jump to conclusions, and I don't want her to jump to any more."

"Did she tell you anything else about what was going on?" Dawson asked.

Jen nodded. "She said earlier that the field hands had found bones—bones that might have been Sheridan's. There are some people who speculate around here that if his bones were dug up, his soul was no longer resting at peace. I don't know if that accounts for wreaking havoc on the plantation, but I'm not sure of anything at this point. I do know this, though: the more time I spend with Monique and Elolie, the harder it is for me to believe that someone like Tom did this."

"What, you think it's voodoo?" Pacey asked.

Jen shrugged. "I told you, I don't know what I think. But Elolie's got her finger on the pulse of this plantation. She always has. Now, she knows something's wrong and Monique believes her, so I'm willing to believe them. But if they can't blame this stuff on Tom, then they have to find out what it is, and they can't do it alone."

"Of course they can't," Dawson said. He looked around the room and knew at once that they were all in accordance. "We're here to help, Jen. I mean, I think we all agree that we can't in good conscience just come here, go to the ball, and split."

"No." Joey shook her head. "Especially now that there seem to be more factors at work. I mean, whether it's voodoo from the past or a crappy person in the present, we've got to work together to get to the bottom of it."

"Thank you, guys. I can't even thank you enough. It's just occurring to me more and more how serious this is, the stuff that's happening to the plantation. It's bigger than Monique and Elolie. I don't know. It might be bigger than all of us," Jen said.

There was no need to comment on what Jen had said to her friends. They already knew that it was true. Clearly there were things at work on this plantation that were far beyond their comprehension. As Dawson looked around at his nervous friends, he was pretty sure that none of them wanted to get involved, either. But he wondered if they would be able to escape what was happening with this family, this troubled young woman, this angry uncle, and the dark and foreboding mansion they lived in. Dawson glanced past Joey out the window, toward the South Wing where Joey had said she'd seen a light. He didn't have any reason to doubt her, he realized.

Dawson cleared his throat and looked at Jen. "Elolie's walking around with candles, huh?"

Jen nodded. "Yes, and muttering to herself. Which I guess isn't that odd." Jen didn't want to give more away about the voodoo practice she had been involved in.

"Was she in Isabella's wing?" Dawson asked, glancing quickly at Joey, who knew exactly what he was getting at.

Jen shook her head firmly. "No way. She feels very strongly about staying out of there at night. She was outside. I don't mean to make it sound dark and scary—Monique says that Elolie's doing white magic blessings for Isabella's spirit. Elolie's afraid that if John Sheridan is restless, Isabella will be too. It's a nice sentiment. Just not the sort of thing you want to run into in the middle of the night."

Dawson nodded at Jen, but his eyes were on Joey. More and more, he found that he had to believe what Joey saw. But if Elolie hadn't been in Isabella's wing, who had? The unspoken question hung in the air over Dawson and Joey.

9

The Mind Is a Battlefield

Pacey woke up with the feeling he'd been through a war. His head was pounding and he could barely open his eyes. He didn't think anyone had slept very well, considering that their evening had ended on such a tense note. He still couldn't believe that Joey had found a snake in her bed, though he had tried to mask his shock the night before.

Pacey had woken up before the others. He couldn't remember the last time he'd had this much trouble sleeping. If anything, sleeping was one of his finer points. He pulled on some clothes, tied his sneakers and slowly, quietly slipped out of the bedroom, tiptoeing past Dawson and Jack. The sun had just barely risen. Pacey eased through the front door of the carriage house and stood on the step, blinking sleepily. The sun was starting to hit the main house, making it look slightly less ominous. Pacey decided to wander inside and see if anyone was stirring yet. He felt antsy, itching to do something. Aside from that, his stomach was rumbling.

He found that the back door, which led into the kitchen, was unlocked. Pacey stepped inside the kitchen and breathed in deeply. Despite the fact that Pacey was wary of Elolie, he couldn't help but appreciate her cooking skills. She must have baked something overnight that made the kitchen smell amazing. There was a sweet, warm smell of cinnamon in the air. As Pacey breathed in, however, he felt another deep stabbing pain in his head and decided he definitely had to look for aspirin.

He found some in the cabinet above the sink and swallowed it down with some water, wincing as the pain in his head suddenly worsened. Suddenly, Pacey slammed the water glass down on the counter. It shattered, slicing Pacey's palm. However, the pain of the headache was so strong that Pacey couldn't focus on his injured hand. He gripped his head with his hands. The throbbing was really intense now, and Pacey squinted, looking out the window, trying to breathe through the pain. When he closed his eyes, he felt like his body had been shocked. He stumbled away from the counter. Behind his closed eyes, a disturbing flash of images raced through his mind. Dust rising off of beaten earth. Horses, rearing up in slow motion, throwing riders off their backs. Men in uniforms, Confederate uniforms. These men were being shot, the bullets raking their bodies, throwing the men to the ground. The soldiers stumbled into each other, screaming, their arms rising up to the sky. Pacey's eyes flashed open. He found he was gripping a chair, and had to sit down. He was shaking, breathing heavily. A fine layer of cold sweat covered his skin. He had no idea what had just happened, but he would consider himself a lucky man if it never happened again. He pressed his head into his hands, trying to calm down. In this position, he didn't hear Elolie come in.

She stood in the doorway of the kitchen for a moment, watching Pacey try to slow his breath. A smile crept across her lips and she said, "The dead speakin' to you now, boy?"

Pacey jumped in his chair. "Jeez, woman. You trying to scare the living dead out of me?"

Elolie threw her head back and laughed. "Sometin' like dat. What's wrong with yo' head?" She smiled again and turned toward the cabinets. She started taking out things, completely ignoring Pacey. Pacey looked down at his hands, which were covered in blood. He tentatively touched his head, which was also blood-smeared. "Oh, man," he whispered.

Pacey stared at Elolie's back for a moment. Was he still sleeping? What the heck had that been back there? He rubbed his eyes again and stood up.

"Why am I still standing here?" Pacey wondered out loud. Elolie merely chuckled to herself again. Then she turned around. She hadn't been ignoring him after all; she'd merely been gathering medical supplies from the cupboard. Without saying a word, she approached Pacey with a first aid kit and tended to Pacey's hand. She silently checked to see if there was any glass in the cut, and then she cleaned it with alcohol and wrapped it in gauze. She gave Pacey a swab to wipe away the blood on his forehead.

"Thank you," Pacey said to her.

Elolie just nodded, and peered into his eyes. "Now ya know," she said. Pacey appreciated Elolie's help, but he wasn't ready to talk to her about what he had seen. Her eyes were too intense for him. He murmured "thank you" again, and hightailed it out of the kitchen.

He didn't want to go back to the carriage house. He needed to clear his head, not to mention the fact he was literally scared out of his mind and couldn't see straight. Pacey didn't even know where he was going. All he knew was that he wanted to walk. He ducked under the overhanging oak branches, moving toward the center of the forest behind the mansion. The foliage was so thick there, dense and mossy, that the sun barely spattered through. Little spots of sunlight here and there danced over the ferns, but for the most part, Pacey felt like he was in a cave. It was damp, and dark. His sneakers were sinking softly into the ground. Pacey looked around him and realized that he must be by the bayou. The mossy banks rolled gently into the swamp.

Pacey looked around for a second. It seemed almost as if the thick cypress trees had closed in around him as soon as he walked through them. He could barely make out the mansion through the trees. He wondered if his friends were awake yet. Would they notice he was gone? Would they think to look for him? Was there quicksand out here that he was going to be sucked into?

"Great. This is just great," Pacey said. He'd had about enough creepiness for one day, and it wasn't even nine o'clock.

Just then, he heard a rustling in the ferns by the swamp. Pacey squinted through the foliage and realized he wasn't alone. A large alligator was making its way slowly along the moist bank of the bayou, its thick, scaly limbs dragging him along. The beast looked prehistoric . . . and hungry. The alligator's dull, yellow eyes rolled slowly to the side and fixed on Pacey. Pacey froze. Now he knew what was meant by the phrase "His heart jumped into his throat."

"Oh, no . . . no, no, no, my friend." Pacey started to inch slowly away from the gator. "I don't look as good as you think," Pacey said. "I'm really stringy. And my diet is . . . well, disastrous. You don't want any part of what I've got going on in here."

The alligator didn't seem to agree. He started moving toward Pacey, his long, muscular tail slashing through the brush. Pacey literally stopped breathing. The swamp seemed to close in on him, the shadows even darker than before. He muttered under his breath, "This has truly not been my day."

Just then, Pacey heard more rustling in the bushes behind him. He was too scared to turn and look, for fear that it was another gator. Were they closing in on him from all sides now? But before he knew it, Jen's cousin, Monique, stepped past him into his line of vision and wrapped her arms around the massive gator. She gently led him back to the bayou bank.

Monique turned around to face Pacey, wiping off her hands on her jeans. She smiled. "That's Sebastian. He was just trying to say hi."

Pacey still couldn't believe his eyes. How had this delicate brunette just marched into the swamp and dragged a gator away? He had never felt like more of a wuss in his life. "Just trying to say hi? Or just trying to digest me?" Pacey asked.

Monique laughed. She seemed slightly more at ease than she had yesterday. She started to walk out of the shadowy marsh, and Pacey, grateful for a guide home, followed her.

"He's the Percy family pet," Monique explained. "He's so old, and has been around this family for so long that he's used to humans and pretty tame."

"Pretty tame?" Pacey asked. "I kinda like my gators a hundred percent tame."

"He won't hurt you," Monique replied. "You're not a threat."

As if to prove the girl's point, Sebastian hauled himself out of the water Monique had returned him to and began trudging along behind them. Pacey certainly found that a little nerve-racking, and glanced at Monique as the beast rustled through the mossy undergrowth.

"Um . . . what did you do, teach the big guy to heel or something?" Pacey asked, regarding the gator's obedience as it moved slowly behind them.

"Pretty much," Monique replied in a fairly deadpan manner. "We thought for a while we might get him on Letterman. You know, stupid pet tricks. That was really my dad's thing, though, and . . . you know."

"Yeah," Pacey nodded, not wanting to make Monique feel like she had to elaborate. "Maybe he could help out with the people who are threatening you, then," Pacey said. "He's as good a watchdog as any. And pretty responsive, right? I mean, look at those choppers."

The two stopped walking for a moment and glanced back at Sebastian, who, on cue, grinned a sly smile, his mouth opening to once again reveal the rows of thick, yellowing teeth.

"See," Pacey said nervously. "That, that's just great."

Monique stopped walking and scanned Pacey's face. It was clear that she still wasn't ready to go into the details of what was going on at her house with just anybody.

Pacey sensed her skepticism, so he added, "You know that we're doing all we can to help out. Although . . . well, I don't know what I'm good for."

Monique smiled. "You're just supposed to concentrate on taking it all in."

Pacey was surprised to find himself laughing. "Oh, is that my role, now? Is that the rumor on the streets?"

"That's the rumor on the streets." Monique nodded. They walked for a moment, and she contemplated the gator. "Maybe he can help," she shrugged. "Positive relationships with animals are a very big part of the voodoo practice."

"I thought the only relationship voodoo had with animals was cutting off their legs and drinking their blood," Pacey said. As soon as it came out of his mouth, he realized how offensive it sounded.

"Yeah, well, it's easy for people who aren't from around here to think that," Monique said. "I wouldn't expect you to understand, but you shouldn't jump to such conclusions. The practice of voodoo does good as well as bad, just like any religion, if you really think about it."

Pacey nodded. "I didn't mean to offend you." He paused, wondering how to work the conversation so that he seemed to be more understanding. After all, he wanted to understand. He just wasn't sure where to begin. The things he was beginning to encounter in New Orleans were new and frightening to him.

"I know you didn't mean to offend me," Monique said, smiling. "I'm just trying to explain to you that there are good sides to voodoo as well. I mean, I grew up with it, with Elolie. It's certainly not all I believe in, but it's part of it. I hadn't ever experienced the bad side, until these bad omens around the plantation. And as for the bones, it started something. Who knows if they legitimately released something, or if something . . . someone bad is out to scare us. Either way, it's not a good thing. "

"You think it's voodoo?" Pacey asked. Though he was skeptical, he wanted to give Monique the benefit of the doubt.

Judging from the look on Monique's face, she obviously sensed his cynicism.

"There's something I think you should understand,

Pacey," Monique began. "Voodoo isn't devil worship, or something that even goes against your idea of God."

"I don't even have much of an idea of God," Pacey admitted.

"Exactly," Monique nodded. "Sometimes we get confused about religion when we're young because it seems restrictive. And it really isn't that cut-and-dried. I'm not saying anything that goes against God—I believe in God."

"But what about the whole idea of casting spells on people and all that stuff?" Pacey wondered.

"Voodoo isn't primarily used to inflict pain on others. Kundalini is the primary force of voodoo. It rises and touches all energy centers of the body. Kundalini is like . . . a river that flows inside of you. Everything you do is to lift yourself to higher consciousness." Monique was getting flushed just talking about it.

Pacey was surprised to find himself interested in what Monique was saying. He hadn't put a lot of thought into his own beliefs on religion, or God. Monique was right; sometimes the notion of concrete beliefs was daunting. There was so much in the universe that couldn't be explained, including what had happened to him that morning, that made Pacey wonder if maybe he should start thinking more about what he believed in. He was surprised to find that he didn't even really know. After all, life had been fairly uncomplicated up until this point, aside from the typical teen angst. Pacey hadn't really given a lot of thought to questioning his place in the universe.

The two had stepped through the clearing at this point. The sun was higher in the sky now, and Pacey squinted against its brightness. His headache was finally starting to fade. He didn't want to say anything to further upset Monique; he was glad to have finally made a connection with her. Still he couldn't help but wonder about what she had told him. A good side to voodoo? He wondered if he should tell his friends about the vision. Would they understand, or would they think he was crazy? He wasn't sure, but the more he talked and learned about voodoo, the more he wondered if it had anything to do with what he was experiencing.

He glanced over to where the carriage house was. He imagined that his friends were stirring inside, but he didn't know if he could put himself back into that reality. Not yet. He turned to Monique.

"Do you mind putting off breakfast a little longer? Maybe walking around? I don't think I'm ready to go back in, yet," Pacey said.

Monique shrugged. "Sure," she said. "If you want to see more of the plantation, I can show you some places where other strange things have been happening."

Pacey was concerned. "Have there really been a lot of incidents?"

Monique nodded. "Oh, yeah. I mean, who knows if they're all related or not, but something's definitely going on, and I don't think it's the Blair Witch."

The two continued to walk away from the mansion, toward the expansive fields of the plantation. He was glad to have found a friend in Jen's cousin.

He felt that perhaps she would be able to understand what he was going through. After all, she'd been raised in a pretty . . . alternative household, and she might be able to offer explanations to what he had already assumed were the inexplicable. They walked beside each other quietly for a while, their feet sinking into the soft ground of the rich plantation. Pacey scanned the green fields, areas of which were now less lush than he assumed they once had been. He hoped, for Monique's sake, that further damage wasn't inflicted on her crops. He wondered if it had in fact been that guy, Tom, they had seen on their first day there. He peered sideways at Monique, who was pointing out a live oak tree with strange slashes in it off in the distance.

"Those trees are part of our legacy," Monique said. "They've been here as long as the Percys have. And now someone's trying to hurt them. I don't know why."

"Do you think it's Tom?" Pacey asked.

Monique was surprised by the question, and she surprised Pacey even more by looking away from him and avoiding the question all together. "Pacey, I don't know what to do. Michael wants me to sell this place."

"Yeah, but he seems to have an agenda with you, right?" Pacey asked. "Maybe he just wants to take care of you and it's his way of helping."

Monique shook her head, hesitating. "It's . . . complicated. We've known each other forever, and I think maybe his feelings for me are . . . different than mine are for him. And I've known Tom all my life, too. . . ." she trailed off, squinting at Pacey. "Why am I even telling you this?" she laughed. She nervously wrapped her long brunette hair into a ponytail. "You don't want to hear this stuff."

Pacey laughed and rocked back on his heels. "Oh, I wouldn't say that. You save a guy from a gator in the bayou, you're bound to get close pretty quickly. Besides, I know how intricate these things get with people you've known all your life. I've known a couple of people back at the house my whole life, and believe me, it certainly gets confusing. I guess it all comes down to who you want to be with at a given point in your life."

Monique smiled at Pacey, appreciating his candor. "Well, that's nice to hear. I guess that there are triangles wherever you go. But it's not quite as simple as who you want to be with. . . ." She stopped again, laughing in embarrassment. "You know, I really am talking about this too much. It's just—will you do me a favor, Pacey, and not mention what I've said to you? About the guys, I mean. There's nothing going on . . . nothing I need to talk about. Wanna just keep walking?"

Pacey nodded. It sounded good to him. Still, he wondered why Monique was so reluctant to talk about Tom. Pacey wondered if Tom had done something to Monique. *Maybe he was jealous of Michael,* Pacey thought. Jealousy was certainly an emotion he could relate to. Pacey didn't know why he was making a soap opera out of people he didn't know. All he knew was that Monique was troubled about something, and he found himself wanting to help her. And he liked walking with her, getting to know more about things at this mysterious plantation.

He certainly didn't feel like being alone with his own thoughts; he was chilled to the bone about what his mind might conjure up.

10

A Method in the Madness

Joey yawned, blinking into the early morning sunlight. Jen was still asleep beside her, and Andie was tangled in her covers, fast asleep on the neighboring bed. Looking at Andie, Joey wondered how Andie got herself so tangled, her covers wrapped around her like a mummy. It looked humanly impossible. How could someone squirm around so much? Squirming, of course, made her think about the snake that had been in her bed the night before. Joey closed her eyes, trying to block out the image of the snake slithering under the covers, but closing her eyes only made it worse. She pressed her lips in determination, opened her eyes, and got out of bed. The light of day was going to make everything better.

As she stepped down on the cold wood floor, she

began to think about everything Jen had told them the night before. About how severe the plantation's financial troubles were and how that somehow was wrapped up in the bones that were discovered. Though Jen had downplayed the bad omens and the rumors that Isabella Percy was seeking her revenge, it had explained the discovery of a snake in their room. Joey looked out the window, studying the mansion. She'd thought she'd seen a light in the South Wing last night. *Could Isabella Percy really be reaching from beyond the grave? Was it possible?* She knew this wasn't a rational thought; it was more something Dawson Leery had put into her head with all those movie nights. There'd been a period of time when he had made her watch every scary movie ever made. Gruesome films with tons of blood, and ominous music, with an occasional spooky house. She felt now like she did then; a false fear filled her heart, knowing that there was a logical explanation to everything.

"Morning." Joey nearly jumped out of her skin when she heard the voice. "Jumpy much?" It was Andie.

"You just startled me, that's all." Joey began to feel silly. There was no such thing as ghosts who used voodoo for revenge, or ghosts, for that matter.

"I'm starving. Want to get something to eat before we save the world?" Andie tried to motion toward the door, but couldn't move her hands.

"How 'bout we get you out of that mess first," Joey offered.

"Thanks. I told you I tossed and turned in my sleep."

"That's some tossing and turning." Jen was now awake, trying to stifle a giggle, but to no avail. Andie just looked too damn funny to her.

"She who laughs . . ." Andie started to laugh, ". . . laughs a lot. Get me out of here." Jen got a mischievous look in her eye that Joey totally understood. They quickly pounced on Andie, and pulled at the covers. "Wait a minute. Not so fast!" Andie unwound like a Yo-Yo, going plop on the floor. This caused even more laughter. The girls couldn't stop. Soon Dawson and Jack joined them.

"What's goin' on?" Dawson stared at the pile o' girls in the middle of the room.

"Looks like a dog pile to me," and Jack dove on top of them, trying to squash them, the girls laughing and rolling under him. Dawson laughed, watching the mass of tangled arms and legs, until Joey jumped on top of him, pulling him down into it. It was nice to have a bit of comic relief, after everything that had happened the night before.

When everyone finally stopped giggling, and the pile dissolved to a one-story row of smiling faces, Andie noticed they were missing a face. "Where's Pacey?"

"Probably went to the main house for breakfast. Witter hunger pains wait for no one, crisis or not." Joey wasn't saying anything that everyone wasn't thinking.

"We should probably all get dressed and figure out what we're going to do," Jen said, hopeful that someone had a plan.

"Why don't we discuss it over breakfast—that is, if Pacey hasn't eaten everything," Dawson suggested.

"Sounds good to me." Jen grabbed a towel and headed into the bathroom, closing the door. Joey and Andie stared after her.

"What's wrong with you guys?" Dawson asked.

"She's going to be in there forever," Andie said matter-of-factly.

"Don't you think you're exaggerating just a little bit?" Dawson said.

"No, she's going to be in there forever," Jack said. "Trust me, I lived with her."

"Fine. You guys can use our bathroom," Dawson offered.

"What makes you think they're going to be any quicker?" Jack asked.

"You are so dead," Andie told him, then pounced, tickling him again. Joey joined in. Dawson just shook his head and went to change.

An hour later Jen came out to an empty room. Her hair was wet, but aside from that she was ready to go. "It's all yours, guys. Guys?" She saw the clock. "Wow." Even she didn't think she was this slow. She quickly rushed to the main house.

In the kitchen, dirty plates littered the breakfast table where Dawson, Joey, Andie, and Jack sat in deep discussion. As the screen door slammed shut behind Jen, she suddenly felt more than late. "What's goin' on? And where's everyone else?"

"We came in to an empty house, but breakfast was waiting. It's all sort of weird, but I figure it's par for the course, right? Though I'm getting this creepy feeling that someone is watching us—I know, it's my imagination." Jack pulled out a chair for Jen. "Anyway, plant it, Lindley. The man's got a plan."

Jen looked at Dawson, the man with a plan. He stared back at her, shrugged. "After what you said last night, I couldn't sleep. Between the snake in your bed—"

"Let's not talk about things that slither in the night. Actually, let's not talk about things that slither at all, unless they happen to be ex-boyfriends," Jen said.

"Look at the bright side. At least it wasn't poisonous," Andie offered. Joey glared at her. That definitely didn't make her feel any better.

"Jen, someone is obviously trying to scare us. And the question is, why? How could we possibly threaten anyone?" Dawson knew that they were missing some vital piece of the puzzle, and he was determined to find it. "Joey, Pacey and I are going to take a look around and search for any kind of incriminating evidence. We thought you could go with Andie and Jack into town." Jen looked confused. "Andie has this great idea."

"I worked last summer at the Capeside Historical Society, and I think with the right paperwork, we could definitely declare this place a historical landmark. We're going to need the family genealogy book." Andie looked fairly optimistic.

Jen smiled, "I happen to know where that is. Does Monique know what we're doing?"

Dawson explained that he didn't want to raise Monique's hopes until they had something solid, so they'd fill her in at the end of the day.

Jen had to admire how Dawson dealt with things. He was always good at helping someone in trouble. Last year, he'd even risked his life, stealing a boat and coming out in a hurricane to save Pacey and her. Jen would never forget that. "Dawson Leery, your white horse act is quite charming." Jen said this flirtatiously, but it was actually more admiration than anything else. She knew that if anyone could figure a way out of this for her cousin, it was Dawson.

The screen door slammed again, and everyone turned around. Pacey stood there, not looking so great.

"What happened to you?" Joey blurted out. "You look like you've seen a—" Joey stopped abruptly. She felt silly for even using the phrase.

"Not exactly that, Joe." Pacey went on to recount his vision in detail. "I just keep getting these headaches that are more nightmare than headache. I saw a black horse, like the one that's supposed to signal the apocalypse. It reared on its hind legs, and threw off its rider. Clouds of red dust came off the ground as more horses rode into cannon fire. The flash of powder. The smoke from the guns. Bodies on the ground, and blood. Everywhere. On everything."

Jack wondered if Pacey had actually slept.

"I know what a nightmare is. And that was definitely not. I think it has to do with that curse Elolie put on me yesterday. I've got to find her." But he couldn't move. "Which I could actually do if she wasn't so damn creepy."

Jen put a hand on his shoulder, reassuring him

that Elolie would never do anything bad to him. She didn't deal in black magic. Jack wanted to know how she could be so sure. Jen couldn't explain it. She just felt it.

The clock struck ten. It was time to get started if they were going to do Monique any good. Jen hugged Pacey, telling him she was sure he was going to be okay, then headed into the library. Andie and Jack followed her. That left Dawson and Joey with Pacey.

"So, what now?" Pacey wanted to know.

"Go talk to Elolie already. You can catch up with us when you're through," Joey said to him reassuringly.

"Where are you guys going?" asked Pacey.

"There's got to be some evidence out there somewhere about who's behind this. Because as much as everyone wants to believe in ghosts and voodoo, I've got to believe it's something more." Dawson started for the door. "You comin', Joe?"

Joey looked at Pacey. She knew he was scared, and wondered if she should leave him alone.

Pacey smiled at her then, and winked. "Don't worry about me. I'm fine."

Joey, taking him at his word, followed Dawson out the door. The screen door slapped shut behind them, and Pacey watched them until they disappeared from his view, wondering what they would find.

Within ten minutes they'd made their way to the stables and began to snoop around. "Dawson, you were here when Caleb said it was Tom Griffin's fault.

What are we looking for?" Dawson didn't answer her; instead he started to scale the horse pen. Joey stood below him; she thought that climbing over the fence seemed dangerous. The pen was high and the horses inside could easily scare and charge him. They were already restless, pushing their bodies against the railing, all in a big cluster.

Dawson told her he thought Caleb might have overlooked something, then slowly dropped into the pen.

"Be careful," was the only thing Joey could get out, covering her eyes.

Dawson smiled at her as his feet touched bottom. He had to admit she looked adorable, hand over her eyes, peeking more than not through her fingers, then slowly lifting them from her face.

"What are you smiling at?" Joey wanted to know.

"You." Dawson was still staring at Joey when he felt a wet mouth on his ear. The horse he had ridden yesterday was reacquainting itself. Joey and he shared a laugh, then Dawson began to circle the pen looking for any kind of clue that could still be left. When they got to the far side of the stable Dawson spotted something under some hay. He dug it out. It was a small doll with a lock of raven hair pinned to it.

"More voodoo. Even looks like Monique. Someone obviously is determined to scare her," Joey said.

"The question is still—who? Let's go check on the bones." He scooped the doll and hair into his pocket and scaled the fence once again.

The bones were in the barn. As they got closer to the structure, they noticed a circle of powder that went all the way around its perimeter. They could see the plow was just inside its door, and next to it sat the skull and a few bones, all neatly stacked.

"What do you make of that?" Dawson didn't understand the circle.

"You're the big horror buff, you tell me." Joey stared at Dawson, who was taking a bit of the white powder in his hands and smelling it. He sniffed again. Joey could see that he overdid it. He was crinkling his nose, trying to suppress a sneeze.

"Hey, Sherlock, you okay?" Dawson nodded. "So what is it?" Joey asked.

"My guess is white magic. Jen did talk about Elolie and her spells. If she's trying to contain Sheridan's spirit, this would make sense." Dawson picked up the skull and studied it, then the bones.

"And maybe this is all a ruse. We need proof and motive," Joey said.

He smiled at her then, knowing how logical Joey always was, and said they should check out the south side, since it was where all the talk of voodoo and Isabella Percy's revenge began. If they were going to find anything, it would be there. They began to walk. The sky was a remarkable blue, not a cloud in sight. The grass was green and wet, sticking to the tops of their shoes as they walked. Dawson genuinely believed they would find something there that pointed a finger at someone. And even if everything pointed at the supernatural, they would find a solution. He knew this in his heart. Every horror movie he'd ever seen, which was basically all of them, had a way to defeat the villain, even if it were supernatural.

They walked over a small hill to find acres that had been plowed but not planted. Weeds were now beginning to take. The ground was hard, and there were piles of dirt everywhere. So this was where the bones had been found. As they looked to the left they could see a stake, with something small bobbing from it. Dawson knew it was the shrunken head. It obviously hadn't been removed, which meant it served its purpose—to scare everyone and perpetuate this myth, if it was a myth.

"Joe, you don't have to come over here," he told her as he made his way toward it.

"Contrary to popular belief, I am not a big chicken. I can handle it." She kept pace with him, trying to not show that she was spooked. She didn't want to think it could be real, but anything was possible.

The small head twitched in the wind, slapping against the large wooden stake that seemed to only serve as an anchor. As they got closer, Dawson studied the head, thinking it really looked real, then reached out to touch it—

"No! What do you think you're doing?" Joey couldn't believe he almost touched that thing.

"I'm just examining it. It's no big deal." He reached out again hesitantly, and then took it in his fingers, looking at the small face that was contorted in pain. Joey found that it was hard to keep her eyes trained on it. She was getting goose bumps on her arms, and wanted to run. It was the same feeling she got every summer when she saw ants swarm and devour some poor dead animal on the road. After a few moments she couldn't take it anymore.

"So?" she said, looking at the ground.

"It's not going to bite."

When she looked up he was holding the head right in front of her. "Jesus. Get that thing away from me!"

"I thought you said it wasn't real."

"It's not." She didn't say it with as much conviction as she would have liked. Dawson slowly turned the head upside down, trying to see where it'd been severed from a neck. "It's not, right?" she asked, not really wanting to know suddenly.

Dawson studied it a bit more. "I think it's a real head."

"So what now?"

"We verify it." Dawson put the head into his pants pocket and then forced the stake out of the ground, throwing it down. Even if he thought it were real, which it couldn't be, he wasn't going to continue perpetuating this myth.

"Not to question your authority or anything, but do you really think that was a good idea? I sort of would like to keep my head." Joey said it jokingly, but some part of her wondered if there would be repercussions for what Dawson just did. If this was truly Isabella Percy's head, she didn't want to walk around with it waiting for Isabella to unleash her fury.

Dawson tapped his pocket and said, "C'mon, Joe."

"Where are we going?" she asked, getting more and more uneasy.

"You'll see." His answer didn't make her any more comfortable.

They walked to the far end of the grounds, until

they were at the Percy graveyard. It was strange to think that generations of one family were all buried here.

"Why are we here?" Joey asked, as Dawson scanned headstone after headstone. None of the graves were belowground here either; instead, they were connected to large crypts.

Dawson stepped over some tall grass and seemed to find what he was looking for. He searched around the large brick structure for an entrance. It was Isabella Percy's tomb.

"That is just wrong." Joey watched him thinking that this looked like some bizarre scene from a Wes Craven film. "I don't think we should go in there." But it was too late; Dawson had already stepped inside. Joey hesitantly ventured in, swallowing hard. She didn't know if she could do this.

Inside it was dark and musty. As her eyes adjusted, Joey noticed that moss covered the walls.

"Joe, you're standing in my light. I can't see what I'm looking for." Dawson tried to move her out of the way.

"That's because you're not supposed to be in here. Now let's go." Dawson suddenly stopped, a look of shock covering his face. Was this even possible?

"What's wrong?" Joey asked.

Dawson had found Isabella Percy's skeleton. It was totally intact, except it didn't have a head.

"You've got to be kidding." Joey came over and took a closer look, and then began looking at the floor.

"What are you looking for?" Dawson asked.

"Well, maybe it fell off and is rolling around under here," Joey said.

For a girl who had been really scared, Dawson had to laugh. "Joe, I think I have her head." And he took it out of his pocket, resting it where it should have been. It was much too small now.

"I can't even believe we're having this conversation. If this is supposed to prove to me that Isabella Percy is behind all this, I'm not buying it. It's all scary hocus-pocus stuff. If it were really her, instead of some dime-store novelty, don't you think she'd rain some black plague down on us? The door would suddenly close and roaches would attack." They both suddenly looked at the door, waiting. Nothing happened. "See, revenge is an all-consuming thing, you know. In all the movies the jilted lover tends to do a lot of damage. It's obvious, Dawson, that someone is behind this and will continue to try to scare the Percys until they get what they want." She was saying this for herself as much as for Dawson. Being in Isabella Percy's crypt was really creeping her out.

"Joe, I'm not disagreeing with you, but standing where we're standing, you've got to admit that Isabella Percy could even be behind all of this," Dawson said.

Joey wished that she could disprove what Dawson suggested, but she couldn't. They'd found nothing that said it was Isabella Percy or anyone else behind all the strange things that had been happening. They were exactly where they had started.

That's why a few minutes later, they found themselves in the barn, putting the head and voodoo doll with Sheridan's bones. If these things were created by black magic, at least this would contain it. And if it were something or someone else, then they were sure to find that out soon. Either way, there was no sense in taking chances.

As they walked away from the barn, Dawson hoped his friends were having better luck.

11

A Bundle of Bones

Jen and Andie stood in the middle of Jackson Square wondering what happened to Jack. He'd gone to park the car over fifteen minutes ago. How long could it take to park? They had so much to do, Jen thought. She turned around to find Andie shopping. She'd obviously found a way to pass the time.

Jack walked out of the parking structure, walking straight into a man on stilts juggling fire. A flaming torch flew by his face, so close he could feel the heat. "Whoa." Jack quickly stepped back into the structure, letting the man on stilts pass. *That was close,* he thought, as he watched stilt man disappear down the alley, flames flying. This time Jack stepped out of the structure a little more hesitantly, and quickly exited the alley. As he turned the corner, he was awash in the sights and sounds of the French Quarter. The streets were cobblestoned, and the buildings were mostly wooden with a distinct European flavor, and only three to four stories high. All the upper stories had planter boxes filled with flowers. Jasmine filled the air. Street vendors sold beads, trinkets, T-shirts, and the foods Jack had only read about or seen on the Food Network on *Emeril*. Though he'd just had breakfast, he was salivating. A violinist played Chopin on the corner next to a fortune-teller. Tourists filled the street taking in all the sights and sounds. As Jack tried to pass the fortune-teller, she stuck out her walking stick and stopped him. She wasn't going to let him pass.

"What's the big hurry?" she asked.

Jack stared at this elderly woman. She was somewhere between fifty and one hundred with a huge mole above her eye. Definitely not attractive and not someone he would normally talk to.

"You are among the few that believe," she said. "The dead have already visited you. Told you that something wicked this way comes. Yes? You must tell your friends before it is too late." She put out her hand. Jack stared at her, irritated. He hadn't wanted his fortune read, least of all when it turned out to be bad.

"So I'm supposed to pay you money because . . . why exactly?" Jack asked, not wanting to buy into any of this.

"Because I know you are afraid. You have to tell your friends that they are in danger," and then she laughed wickedly.

Jack didn't think it was funny. "Leave me alone, okay?" The woman leaned in close to Jack.

"If you do not tell them, someone will die," she hissed. Jack couldn't stand it anymore and tried to get away from this woman, maneuvering into the crowd. After a minute he felt he was far enough away from the woman to stop and scour the horizon, searching for his sister and Jen. They were nowhere to be found.

"Amazing, isn't it?" Jen whispered in Jack's ear, teasing him. He jumped, relieved to turn around to her. "This place really is freaking you out."

"No, just this . . ." Jack was about to indicate the fortune-teller, but she'd disappeared. "Never mind." Jack smiled at Jen then, shaking off the tingles. "Where's Andie?"

"Haggling. She saw a scarf she had to have. Then it's off to the Historical Society to save the day, eh, Jack?" Jen felt better about everything now. They were going to be able to help her cousin, so all would be right in the world again.

Jack smiled back. He liked the idea of helping Monique, too. But he also knew his sister. If she bought one thing, she was bound to buy another, and they'd be there all day.

They caught up with Andie, who was just putting on her new purchase, a beautiful turquoise silk scarf, with a multi pattern in it. She tied it loosely around her neck, asking, "So?" Andie asked, then reacted to Jack's frown. "What's wrong? Is it crooked?"

"No, he's just scared you're going to start a shopaholic binge, and we'll have to take you to some twelve-step program." Jen pinched Jack.

"Hey, I didn't say anything. Ladies, ready to hit it?" Jack offered an arm to each and they started down the street. But it was too late; Andie saw things she just had to have.

After three more purchases, Jen noticed a man in a black hooded sweatshirt. She couldn't see his face, but something about him gave her the willies. "Come on guys, let's go." She pulled on Andie, "Let's go, okay?"

"What's the big deal?" Andie asked as they began to walk, Jen quickening their pace. "And what's the hurry?"

Jen hooked her arm in Andie's and whispered to her, "I think we're being followed. Don't turn around." Andie immediately turned around. Jack watched Andie's eyes dart around the crowd, then rest on the man in the black hooded sweatshirt.

"What's going on?" Jack wanted to know.

Jen spotted a cop across the square. "Jack, stay with Andie. I'm just going to go talk to that cop for a minute. I'm sure it's nothing." As Jen walked away from them, she hoped she was right.

Jack and Andie watched as Jen disappeared into the crowd. Andie frowned. In horror movies, wasn't it a bad idea for the group of well meaning kids to split up? She grabbed onto Jack's hand.

"Andie, chill out. It's broad daylight and we're surrounded by people. I'm sure we're fine," Jack said.

"Yeah, just like in *I Know What You Did Last Summer* when the killer showed up at the parade," Andie retorted.

Jack glanced behind them. The man in the black

hooded sweatshirt was still subtly following them, the hood shadowing his face.

"Let's pick up the pace," he muttered to his sister. And then, Jack and Andie did exactly what every movie they had ever seen had taught them not to do when being followed by menacing men in hooded sweatshirts; they got out of the crowd and ducked into an alley.

The tall buildings obscured the sun, making the alley cold and dank. They seemed to be in a warehouse district, but the heavy doors were all chained and locked. Andie looked furtively behind them just in time to see the man in the sweatshirt rounding the corner.

"Jack!" She hissed, clenching onto her brother's arm.

"I know, I know," he said. Jack and Andie started running and then, as if by some miracle, they found a warehouse door that was open. It was barely open enough to squeeze the two of them in, but it was the safest haven they were going to find.

However, the warehouse was not the most inviting place to hide from danger. In fact, it looked like the set of a slasher film. The space seemed to be used for storage for Mardi Gras floats. What were once gorgeous and colorful floats in the parades now seemed grotesque as they loomed over Jack and Andie. Holding on to each other, they crept through the shadows of the looming floats, squinting up at the oversize heads. The faces were painted with bright red, leering mouths and wide, frightened eyes.

Andie shuddered and whispered, "Okay, not only

is it bad enough that we're running from some bizarre hooded man for God knows what reason, but we have to skulk around in some kind of demented funhouse, too?"

Jack nodded. "I can't even think of why this guy would be after us. I mean, maybe we should just give up the chase. We can't possibly have anything he wants."

Andie's eyes widened. "You don't know that, Jack. We're in New Orleans. Maybe he wants to, you know, cut our hearts out or something."

Jack stopped for a moment to stare at his sister. "That is so offensive," he told her.

"You were the one who thought that this place was going to be just like something out of *Angel Heart* or something!" Andie exclaimed.

"Yes, but now I have an open mind," Jack said.

"Well, now is a pretty funny time to be optimistic, what with snakes in the beds and strangers chasing us in the alleys," Andie said.

Jack realized his sister was right. Despite his determination to be brave, Jack felt the need to tell his sister what the old woman had just told him.

"Yeah, about that," Jack said. "This crazy old woman in the street told me that someone going to die, and I had to warn them."

"Jeez!" Andie said. "Well, don't say anything to freak anybody out."

"No, I know," Jack replied. "But on the other hand, what if I'm supposed to say something and I don't and something awful happens?"

The only response Andie had was a look of fear.

Jack and Andie stood still for a moment, just breathing in the dark, ominous space. They heard nothing around them. It seemed that they had lost their stalker, and they both let out a quiet sigh of relief. However, just as they were about to turn around and leave the warehouse, they saw the shadow of a man behind a mass of muslin fabric! Andie screamed, startling Jack. Jack thought fast and dove forward to rip the fabric down, hoping to ensnare the man. Andie jumped forward to help him. It was dark in the warehouse, and the fabric was heavy and laced with thick dust. Andie felt a strong arm grab her in the dark—stronger even than Jack was. She felt as if her heart stopped for a moment, as if she were in a dream where she was being chased and couldn't move. Suddenly, she felt the strap of her bag being yanked down her arm, so harshly that it stung her skin. "Hey!" she screamed. But she couldn't move, couldn't reach through the thick, dusty fabric to stop the man as he yanked her purse off of her arm completely. She screamed again, calling for Jack, but before he knew it, he was tangled in the fabric too, and the man had disappeared!

Jack freed himself, grabbing Andie by the shoulders. Dust from all the movement swirled around them. "Listen, you stay here for a second. He can't have gotten far. I'm running out onto the street."

Before Andie could protest—after all, she didn't exactly feel like staying alone in the dank warehouse—Jack was out the door. Andie's eyes darted around the room. Where on earth had the hooded man gone? It seemed he had disappeared into thin air. But he hadn't disappeared completely. Andie crouched down to the dirty warehouse floor and picked up a small bundle of dried flowers wrapped around small, delicate bones.

Meanwhile, Jack was barely ten feet out of the warehouse door when he ran smack into Michael Stetcher! Jack was breathless, and scared out of his mind to run into another person in the alley. "Hey," Jack said. He didn't know where to even begin, so he started with the basics. "What are you doing here?"

"Winston used to have an antiques store here in the Quarter. It's boarded up now, but he still keeps some books and paperwork there. I was just gathering some work for him, and this is the back way I usually take to cut through town. I saw this guy racing out of here with something that obviously wasn't his. . . ."

Michael held up Andie's bag. Jack's eyes widened. "But this obviously isn't yours either, right?" Michael smiled. "You with Andie?"

"I am," Jack nodded. "She's still inside. Are you . . . how did you . . . ?"

"I grabbed it without even thinking," Michael said. "This stuff happens all the time, unfortunately. I guess I've seen one too many people get ripped off when I couldn't do anything about it. I'm glad that I managed to help someone I actually know. Hooded guy, right?"

"Yeah." Jack nodded, glancing back to where Andie was hiding. "Andie!" He yelled. "It's safe, come on out!"

Andie peered out of the warehouse, blinking in the daylight. "Michael?" she asked.

"He was walking by when the guy came out," Jack said. "He thought fast and grabbed the bag. How awesome is that?"

"Very awesome," Andie agreed. She approached Michael to take her bag, and looked inside. However, she immediately frowned. "That's weird . . . everything's here, my wallet and everything . . . but the genealogy book is missing."

"Are you kidding?" Jack asked.

Andie looked up at Michael again, a shadow passing over her face. "I'm sorry, remind me again of how you just happened to be exactly where we were when a crime just happened?"

"Andie—" Jack interrupted, glancing at Michael.

"I'm not trying to be rude or anything," Andie said earnestly. "You've got to understand, though, it's been a rough morning."

"Look, I understand." Michael shook his head. "It's a wild coincidence, I know. But like I told Jack, Winston's old shop is literally around the corner. I go in there periodically to do some paperwork for him on the past antique auctions and acquisitions, and I really do always take this back alley as a short cut on my way back. I like to avoid the tourists. No offense."

Andie looked at Michael Stetcher for another long moment. "None taken, I'm sure."

"What were you guys doing with Percy's book, anyway?" Michael asked. "I can't believe anyone would let that out of the house."

Andie shook her head, dejected. Michael had just reminded her how awful it was that they had lost the genealogy book. "Long story," she sighed. "We were just trying to help, but looks like we can't now."

Jack tried to comfort his sister. "Come on, Andie, we can still go to the Historical Society."

"I'll walk you guys there," Michael offered. "You must be a little shaken up."

"Okay," Andie agreed. "That's nice, Michael, thank you. But we should try to find Jen."

The trio started to walk back toward the crowds in the Quarter. Andie remembered the bundle she had found in the warehouse and took it out of her pocket. "By the way, do you have any idea what this is?" She showed the boys the dried flowers.

Jack shuddered. "Maybe you shouldn't go around picking that stuff up, Andie."

"Why, what is it?" Andie asked.

"It's a gris-gris," Jack said.

"A what-what?" Andie scrunched her face.

"A gris-gris," Michael said. "It's 'mojo.' You put together specific ingredients, either for good or evil, and bundle them together to cast a blessing or a curse."

Jack sighed. "It's a voodoo thing. Someone's put a spell on us."

"That's why the guy was following us?" Andie asked.

"I guess so. I don't know. That and to snag the book, I guess. This is freaking me out. Put it down and let's get out of here," Jack urged.

"Well, maybe we should keep it for evidence," Andie suggested.

"No way," Jack said. "That's exactly his plan. Maybe hooded sweatshirt guy was planning on us taking this back to the plantation. Maybe he's behind the whole thing."

Michael looked sober. "I'm the last person in the world who wants to freak you guys out, but this definitely isn't a good omen." He paused for a moment, thinking about something. Then he asked, "How's Monique doing in all this? Is she . . . upset?"

Jack and Andie exchanged looks. Yes, Monique had certainly been upset, but they couldn't say specifically if she was upset about being estranged from Michael. It seemed to be the last thing on her mind.

"She's okay," Andie said. "She's been . . . busy." She didn't know why, but she couldn't help but feel bad for the guy when he held such an obvious torch for Monique.

Andie looked at her brother's anxious face, then she glanced at Michael. "Jack, why didn't you tell me about the gris-gris?"

Jack took a moment, really thinking about how to answer. "I don't know," he replied. "Maybe I was scared about what it implied. All I know is that I don't have that many good reasons to not believe in . . . things I might have once scoffed at, if you know what I mean. Come on, let's keep going."

It seemed that events of the past half-hour were like a dream. In fact, Andie didn't feel unlike Dorothy stepping out of the tornado-wrecked house into the colorful world of Oz. She looked at Jack as they walked with Michael up the alley.

"Did that just happen?"

Jack nodded in the affirmative. They were now in the crowd again, still shaking off the creepy feeling that they were being followed. Jen suddenly broke through a throng of people, flushed, her eyes wide.

"Where on earth did you guys go?" Jen asked, out of breath. "I've been racing all over the market looking for you."

"Yeah, well, we were trying to avoid the scary man in the hooded sweatshirt," Jack said.

"I know!" said Jen. "I was trying to find a cop, but he said he was looking for a purse snatcher who I guess has been wreaking havoc this season. I swear he thought I was a paranoid tourist or something."

"Well, yeah, I am a paranoid tourist," Andie said. "After that debacle, who wouldn't be? And my purse *was* snatched, by the way. It's probably the same guy!"

"Are you serious?" Jen asked in concern. "Isn't that your bag you have right there?"

"Yes," Andie said. "Michael got it back for me, amazingly. But the genealogy book is missing."

Jen's face fell. "Okay, well, that's a little more than suspicious. Maybe we should track the cop down and tell him. I'm willing to bet it's the same guy." Jen said.

Jack shook his head. "He's going to think it sounds even crazier than when you originally talked to him. Mysterious hooded man follows kids into warehouse, disappears behind fabric, leaving behind a gris-gris."

"A what-what?" Jen asked.

"It's a voodoo thing," Jack sighed. "We're all doomed."

"It's not that dramatic," Michael said, trying to be soothing. "I'm just trying to warn you guys that something is definitely going on, and I didn't want you to be in danger of looking at things through rose-colored glasses."

"Rose-colored glasses?" Jen snorted. "I think I ground mine into the grass the minute we got out of the car."

Jen turned to face Jack. "And as for you, what's with you being the expert on the scary curse stuff? You've seen this . . . thing before, and you didn't say anything?"

Jack shook his head. "Look, Caleb the wacky old field hand seemed very insistent that I not say anything about it, and frankly, at the time I didn't want to go against him. He seemed pretty freaked out. But this gris-gris . . . it's authentic. I should have told you about it earlier."

"Regardless," Jen said. "It probably wouldn't have helped us today. We wouldn't have known what to look for."

Andie nodded in agreement. "Now we just know to keep our eyes open."

The foursome decided that since there was apparently nothing more they could do about the strange events of the afternoon, they should continue on to do what they originally planned; visit the Historical Society.

As they walked, Jen looked up at Michael. She

hadn't gotten a chance to really speak with him, what with all the drama that had been tangled in their visit. He seemed so much older. Obviously, they had all grown up, but Michael seemed to carry more of an adult weight on his shoulders than the rest of them.

"So, Michael," Jen said softly. "Why do I get the feeling that you know stuff about Monique that you're not telling me?"

Michael laughed quietly. "Same old suspicious Jenny. Look, the only thing I know about Monique is that she's in danger of losing her land if she doesn't take my advice."

"That sounds pretty self-serving, if you ask me," Jen replied.

"Quite the contrary. My only motivation is to help her." Michael paused. "I mean, let's face it, Jen. You know how I feel about Monique. And she might not return that yet, but . . . I've always loved her, always will."

"So you think if you save the day . . ."

"Maybe," Michael said.

"Well, let me tell you, you're not saving anyone trying to convince those two to sell," Jen said.

"Maybe, maybe not. I'm just doing what I think is best."

Jen let it lie there, walking quietly beside this young man she'd known since she was a girl, and now felt she hardly knew at all.

Jack, Jen, Andie, and Michael trudged into their final destination, a pristine white building that looked not unlike Tara from *Gone With the Wind*.

The woman sitting behind the front desk looked as if she had been there since about the same time the classic film had been made. She gazed at the three friends over her bifocals, blinking as slowly as a turtle.

"Yes," the woman sighed. The plaque on her desk indicated that she was Bernice Roberts, the secretary of affairs at the Historical Society.

Andie approached the desk with confidence. "Hi, we're here to declare a landmark."

Bernice nodded slowly. Obviously, she heard this very statement several times a day. "Good for you." She smiled, revealing a set of dentures. "What is it?"

Andie glanced at the others. "The Percy Plantation. I had brought the genealogy book with me to show you, but unfortunately it was stolen on my way here. But this gentleman standing beside me has known the family all his life and can vouch that the Percys have been in this town since the turn of the—"

Bernice held up her hand to signal Andie to stop. "Was there a battle there?" she asked.

Andie glanced at Michael and Jen, who shrugged. "Well, not a battle. A massacre kind of, but soldiers were there to protect—"

"Soldiers were stationed in every plantation during the war. The city was overrun with them." Bernice disappeared under her desk for a moment and reappeared with a sandwich. Clearly, she wanted these young people to leave.

"What about Confederate gold?" Bernice continued, taking a bite into her ham and Swiss.

Andie was dismayed. She had no idea this would be such a losing battle, and she had truly wanted to help Jen's cousin. "Um, no, not that I know of."

Jen was exasperated. "If there was Confederate gold, we wouldn't be in this mess, would we? Look, Bernice, my cousin is about to lose her home. The Percys are one of the oldest families in this town—"

Bernice nodded. "I know that, miss. But unfortunately for you, all of the oldest families in this town are still in this town. If you put all those houses together, it adds up to a whole lot of nothing. Diamonds don't look so special when you're eating them like cereal for breakfast, if you know what I mean."

"Okay, give us the lowdown," Jack said. He had to admit, he was frustrated. This trip into town hadn't proved to be the pleasant diversion he had hoped for. In fact, it just seemed to be further proof that his suspicions were right. He had meant it when he told Andie that he was planning on keeping an open mind, but everything he was letting in was only scaring him more. It seemed like he and his friends were in some sort of trouble here. Worse, it seemed that their plan to help Monique was proving to be completely unsuccessful.

"The lowdown," Bernice sighed, "is that there are approximately 305 historical landmarks in New Orleans proper alone. We can't just slap a plaque on any old house. I appreciate the long line of Percys in this town, but, no famous generals, no hidden gold, no documents signed on the premises, et cetera, nothing I can do for you kids."

They turned to Michael as they trudged out of the building.

"Any bright ideas?" Jen asked Michael.

Michael sighed. "Look, I was completely willing to back you guys up in there . . . but believe me, I want the best for Monique, and I've already looked into ways to save the plantation for her. It's not happening. She's got to sell."

Jen found herself wanting to slap Michael across the face. How could he be so negative about something he knew they were all trying so hard to accomplish?

Jack, Jen, and Andie looked at each other in dismay. This was certainly not the kind of news they'd been hoping to take back to the Percy Plantation.

12

Something Wicked This Way Comes

Back at the plantation, Pacey, who was still mentally exhausted from the morning's events, finally caught up with Elolie. He had to admit that perhaps he hadn't been looking for her that hard, since he was afraid of what a conversation with her would reveal. Still, he didn't want to wake up with more horrifying images like the one he'd had that morning.

Elolie was carrying in freshly picked vegetables from the garden. Pacey rushed to meet her at the kitchen door to hold it open for her. "Hey there, Elolie," Pacey said, a bit too chipper. Elolie grunted in reply, but Pacey still followed her into the kitchen. He watched Elolie spread the carrots and potatoes on the wooden counter.

"So . . . cooking up a stew?" Pacey asked.

Elolie glanced at Pacey crossly. Pacey, suddenly convinced that Elolie was powerful enough to get into his mind with the blink of an eye, jumped toward the counter to help chop the vegetables. Elolie hid her smile as she handed Pacey a knife to slice the potatoes with.

Pacey realized that Elolie wasn't going to start talking, not unless he prompted her. He couldn't believe that he was actually thinking she might have had something to do with the disturbing image he'd had that morning; he had been in steadfast denial of the supernatural. Still, he would do anything to avoid having another run-in with his inner psyche. Pacey took a deep breath and dove in, looking sidelong at Elolie as he spoke.

"So . . . it sure is different from home here," Pacey began. "Some of it's obvious. You know, weather, accents . . ."

"Mmmm-hmmm," Elolie sighed.

"Other stuff is . . . pretty extreme. Like the way I sleep down here. I woke up with this splitting headache this morning. And, um . . . this is going to sound weird, but it got so bad at one point I had to sit down, because the pain was so bad. . . . um . . . it was so bad, I think I started seeing things."

Elolie stopped cutting the carrots and looked at Pacey. There was a long silence. Elolie's amber eyes seemed to flicker like a fire as she gazed at Pacey. Pacey felt himself starting to panic, an ache suddenly throbbing in his head. Where were his friends?

"Well," Elolie finally said, the annoyance in her

voice adding a singsong tone to her words. "Do you know or do you think you know?"

"That I saw something?" Pacey asked. Elolie nodded at him. "Well, I—" Pacey stopped for a moment. Against his will, he remembered the horrible images he had seen that morning. The blood flying. The soldiers being dragged through the dirt. The screams so shrill, so vivid, it seemed they were happening right next to him. Pacey shook his head, snapping back into reality. He was starting to sweat.

"Okay," he said. "Okay. I know. I know I saw something."

Elolie smiled at him as if he were a child who had brought home a paper with gold stars. Then she frowned, like a mother who didn't want her child to think he'd gotten away scot-free.

"You think I don't know what happen? Why you break the glass, run out the kitchen? You think I don't know what you thinkin'?"

Pacey gulped. "No, on the contrary, ma'am, I'm afraid you know exactly what I'm thinking."

"Good dat you can say it out loud. Just wanted to hear you say it out loud."

"So what does that mean?" he asked her.

Elolie shrugged. "Dat your job. The mind opens to reveal what's already there."

Pacey bit his tongue, about to accuse Elolie of being about as helpful as a fortune cookie. However, despite whatever reasonable explanation he tried to come up with to explain his current condition, he kept coming back to the undeniable fact that Elolie had something to do with it. He didn't want to cross

her. He stared down at his pile of raw, sliced potatoes.

"Great. So, do you, uh, need more help with dinner?" Pacey asked. A sly smile spread across Elolie's
face. She turned away from Pacey and opened the
refrigerator, from which she produced a headless
chicken with the feathers intact. She then dipped it
into a pot of already boiling water. Pacey stared,
aghast. She held it out to Pacey with a grin.

Pacey's stomach turned. He covered quickly.
"That's cool. I've been fishing. Same thing, right?
Just take off those, um, pesky feathers?" Elolie nodded, obviously laughing at him as Pacey set the
warm, feathered chicken onto the counter and proceeded to rub the feathers off. Elolie watched over
him.

"Not bad," she said. "You're natural."

"That's good," Pacey said. "Because I don't know
how much else is going to work out for me. Five
years down the line, you mind if I come back here
and maybe be your dish boy or somethin' . . ." Pacey
trailed off as he found himself getting into one of his
least favorite topics of thought: his future. He didn't
like to think too far into the future, considering that
he still didn't know what was going to happen with
his life, with his career. At this point, nothing
seemed too farfetched. He very well could end up
peeling carrots next to this woman. Pacey still
couldn't decide if that was a bad thing or not. It
seemed such a simple thing, just deciding what
would make you happy. But the older he got, the
more complicated gaining simple happiness seemed.

"Sssshhhh." Elolie hushed him. "Best not to talk during preparation. Too much clouding. Take some." She held out a small plastic baggie with crushed herbs inside.

"What is that?" Pacey asked. It didn't look like your run-of-the-mill oregano and rosemary.

Elolie squinted at him. "Shhh," she said again. "For chicken. Spread it on, and keep your mouth shut." She grabbed a handful of the strange herbs and sprinkled it on the chicken like fairy dust. As she rubbed the herbs into the chicken's cavity, she began a low, indecipherable chanting. It sounded similar to when she had pressed her hands on Pacey's temples. Panicked, Pacey started to move away from the counter. Elolie grabbed his hand, stopping him.

"Don't leave in the middle. Bad luck. Get your grip, boy." She squinted at Pacey, annoyed. Pacey gulped. Elolie peered at him. "You scared?" she asked. Pacey nodded, and Elolie leaned in closer. "Sometin's goin' on here. You know it. Pay attention. Sometin' evil. There's black magic here, and it ain't mine. You pay attention."

Pacey felt like someone was running an ice cube across the back of his neck. Startled, he didn't know how to react but to reach into the bag of herbs and continue spreading it on the chicken. This seemed to satisfy Elolie, and she continued with her chanting.

Pacey was so engrossed with the strange dinner preparation that he didn't hear Dawson and Joey walk into the house. They paused in the kitchen doorway for a moment, looking on in shock and amusement as Pacey tossed extra herbs on the skin, tentatively rubbing it in as Elolie murmured her voodoo blessing.

"Whoa," Dawson whispered. "You leave Pacey alone for one afternoon and suddenly he's a steadfast follower."

Joey wrinkled her face, trying not to laugh. "I don't know, Dawson. Pacey's not himself, is he? This whole place is bizarre."

"Not bizarre," Dawson said. He searched for the words. "I just feel like this whole place is shrouded in mystery. Or voodoo, for that matter. From the dinner preparations, to everything we're seeing on the plantation."

"And what exactly are we seeing on the plantation?" Joey asked.

Dawson shook his head. "I know we didn't find anything that pointed to anyone in particular, just that someone is practicing voodoo, and obviously not the kind of voodoo that's going on in this kitchen."

Joey looked up at Dawson. She felt like she could read his mind. "Something darker?" she asked him.

Dawson looked down at Joey. He didn't want to scare her, but he knew that she already knew what he was thinking. Something sinister. He couldn't put his thumb on it. Suddenly he knew that Joey hadn't been imagining things the other night. He was sure that she had seen someone in the forbidden wing of the house. The question was, why would someone be wandering where they didn't belong, and who would cause harm to this family? His mind wan-

Bayou Blues

dered again to the deal that Isabella had with Marie Laveau. He looked at Joey and could tell that she knew his wheels were turning.

"That whole story . . . you know, about Isabella Percy having a deal with Marie Laveau . . ." Dawson said.

Joey nodded. "Yes?"

"Do you think their arrangement really had staying power? I mean, do you really think it's possible that Isabella Percy is upset because Sheridan's bones were disturbed?" Dawson asked.

Joey took a long moment to think about that. "Dawson, I don't even know where to begin in answering that. I mean, this is uncharted territory here. I guess . . . just think about the arrangement."

"That she would be united with John, no matter what," Dawson said.

"No matter what," Joey repeated. She and Dawson looked at each other intensely for a moment, the unspoken hanging between them. Then Joey broke the moment and shrugged. "I can't claim to know anything about the way this voodoo works, Dawson. All I know is that these women both existed, and Marie Laveau seems to have clout beyond the tourist traps, you know?"

"Well, look at you playing Mulder to my Scully," Dawson smiled.

Joey laughed. "Five minutes later, the tables will be turned."

"Well," Dawson sighed, realizing that Pacey and Elolie still hadn't noticed them, and that there was

149

no need to interrupt them. "Looks like they've got dinner handled. You wanna go back to the carriage house and wait for the others until dinner?"

Joey nodded. "Yeah, I'm actually pretty beat from the day."

As the two walked back to the carriage house to await their friends, Dawson wondered if all their hard labor would ever amount to anything. He liked to think that it would, to some degree. The alternative was too unpleasant to think about. The alternative was that whatever was happening to disrupt the plantation and Monique's life on it was bigger, darker, and beyond their control. It might be something none of them could beat, or worse, it might be something that could beat them. Dawson tried to shake the thought as he walked in step with Joey, but the hairs were rising on the back of his neck. He glanced around to see if something was behind him, but he saw only the looming, dark windows of the mansion gaping at him as they walked away. Dawson glanced at Joey and sped up a little. He didn't even know what he was trying to get away from. He was just trying to shake the feeling of something being two steps behind him, just close enough to touch his shoulder.

When Dawson and Joey stepped inside the carriage house, they saw Jack, Jen, and Andie sprawled about in the girls' room. Dawson and Joey stopped short in the doorway.

"Judging by the looks on your faces, I gather today wasn't the most successful of days," Joey said.

Jen only chuckled; a chuckle that died away into a

sad sigh. "We'll tell you the details later, but yeah, it pretty much sucked."

Andie sat up, looking curious. "Hey, where's Pacey, anyway? I thought he was with you guys."

Dawson shook his head. "Nope. He's in the kitchen with Elolie."

Andie squinted. "That sentence is wrong on so many levels."

Joey laughed. "I know, but I think he's actually realized that Elolie can help him."

Jen nodded. "Well, you know, she probably can, though I wasn't sure Pacey would believe me."

"Oh, he's a smart guy," Dawson grinned. "He's not going to be building any shrines on his own any time soon, but still . . ."

Jen groaned. "God, I'm too depressed to even think about this right now. What am I going to tell Monique? I don't even know what's going on here. I feel like there's something lurking around every corner, something breathing down my neck in the dark—"

But before Jen could finish, every single person in the room said, "Me too." The statement said in unison was enough to send them all into a long silence.

"Okay," Jen finally said. "Well, I think this definitely means we should take a pre-dinner nap. You know, collect ourselves. I don't want to be all freaked out and depressed in front of Monique and Uncle Winston."

Dawson nodded, collapsing on the other bed. "I'm up for that," he said.

The six friends settled into the beds, arranging

themselves and snuggling closer for comfort. Their usual antics and banter were momentarily gone. Instead, they gazed up in silence as the long shadows slid across the ceiling of the carriage house, suddenly feeling very much alone in this strange city, with the Percy mansion casting an ever-growing shadow across them.

13

A Light in the Window

Dinner was very quiet that evening, so quiet that Uncle Winston wanted to know what was going on. It wasn't natural for teenagers to be so silent. The gang looked at Jen, who knew she was supposed to say something—but what? The whole situation broke her heart. The idea that Monique would lose her home was more than horrible. Uncle Winston was waiting for some sort of explanation. When Jen opened her mouth nothing came out.

After another uncomfortable moment, Dawson tried to relieve the tension. "I think we're kinda quiet because we don't know what to do. I mean, we thought we did, but we weren't very successful."

"What are you talking about?" Monique didn't understand what Dawson was getting at.

"We thought we could actually help. Dawson, Joey, and Pacey tried to find clues today that would point in some direction to who was responsible for all the weird things happening here, and Jen, Jack, and I . . . well, we tried to get the Percy Plantation declared a historical landmark," Andie explained. "But none of it worked. We found nothing that pointed out who could be behind the strange incidents at the house, and then we also managed to get the Percy genealogy book stolen. We were going to use it to get the land-mark designation."

"We were told even if we had it, it wouldn't have helped," Jen chimed in. "You know, Mo. If it weren't for Michael, Andie would have lost her purse."

Something struck Dawson as funny. "Wait a minute," he said, "The only person who's offered you anything for your home is your friend Michael, right?"

"What are you getting at?" Monique asked.

"What are the chances of having someone you know randomly show up and grab your purse from a thief? He's had access to your place, and you've said his father is a land mogul. Do you think . . ."

Monique stared at Dawson in shock.

"Son, while I'm glad you're not suggesting it's Isabella Percy behind all our mishaps, like my young charge would like to believe, I find it hard to swal-low that Michael is behind any of this. He's practi-cally a member of this family," Winston said.

"I'm not accusing him, sir. I'm just trying to find a

motive for anyone. After all, during that fight, you thought Tom Griffin had motive, and after firing him, isn't it possible that now he'd have even more motive? I'm sorry, I'm not trying to stir up a hornets' nest. Just trying to find out who's behind all of this," Dawson concluded.

Monique began to think about Michael and all the things that had happened over the last month. That seed of doubt was enough for her to question everything about him. Where she'd only been angry with him before, now there came the big "Why?" and she wanted that question answered. Could it really be him? She physically felt sick to her stomach and excused herself from the table.

They all watched her go, Dawson feeling horrible for even planting a seed of doubt. He knew how he would feel if someone had said that about Joey. Winston Percy obviously still thought it was Tom Griffin. After all, he did find the voodoo doll in the stables with what looked like Monique's hair. Tom had stolen the locket, why not other possessions? But they still had no real evidence that pointed to anyone. As far as the field hands were concerned, Isabella Percy's ghost was still hard at work, seeking her revenge for preventing her reunion with John Sheridan. With no real culpable suspect, they would have to figure a way to trap whoever was behind everything. They ate the rest of their meal in silence, wondering what to do next.

It was particularly dark that night. The moon was just a sliver in the sky as the kids made their way back to the carriage house. Pacey kicked at the ground, dust rising around his shoes. Not that he could see it. The only thing any of them could really see were the lights from the carriage house ahead of them, and the lights from the Percy kitchen behind them; maybe a few fireflies. Jen reached out to touch the dancing light in front of her, which flitted away. *Magic,* she thought. Her mind wandered back nine or ten years, to the summer Monique's mother read them *Peter Pan.* It was the summer she learned to believe in magic, to let her mind go. Magic had been good then. It had saved Peter Pan's life. The magic here with them now was the complete polar opposite. It seemed to only promise death and destruction.

"Do you ever wish you were little again?" Jen asked them.

Jack, who was closest to her, said, "Who doesn't? We used to take these great family trips—"

"—Summers in Maine where the mosquitoes and black flies would eat you alive. Especially Tim," Andie said with a sad wistfulness.

"There's something to be said about the sweet days of youth," Dawson smiled at them.

"Spoken by the man who lived with Ward and June. I wouldn't go back if someone paid me." Pacey's childhood wasn't exactly a storybook. "Why the sudden sense of nostalgia, Lindley?"

"Just thinking about when magic was good, and wasn't evil."

"It depended on who used it. Merlin versus Morgana . . ." Dawson started.

Pacey cut in, "—Superman versus Lex Luthor.

Batman versus the Joker, Penguin, Mr. Freeze. If only they'd learned to use their power for the greater good." They were now at the carriage house, and Pacey was grinning like a Cheshire cat.

"Besides the fact that you can never find a super-hero when you need one," Joey said with the same grin on her face. "I guess I'm going to have to settle on one of you. Volunteers? Okay, then . . . Dawson, you've got boogie man duty." She grabbed him by the hand and led him into the girls' room.

"If there's anything in our bed this time, don't tell me." Jen remembered how much safer she'd felt in the carriage house before the snake.

Joey opened the door to the room and flipped on the lights. So far, so good. Everything looked normal. Of course, everything had looked normal the night before, until she turned down the covers. Dawson watched Joey's face. She was bracing herself for the worst, which made him want to get this over with. He'd do anything to protect her, even though Joey was probably the strongest person he knew. Okay, maybe not physically strong, that would be his father, but emotionally, she was one tough cookie.

"Step back, Joe. Just in case." He flipped back the covers—nothing. He looked under the bed, and Joey cringed, her thoughts once again on scary movies. Nothing under there either. Andie's bed. Nothing. And finally, the closet. As Dawson opened the door, something leaped out at him.

"Dawson!" Joey could barely breathe.

Dawson swatted the object as it hit him, trying to

protect himself. It was only an old hat box. Joey breathed a sigh of relief. They both did. Dawson held up his attacker. "So much for the boogie man."

They gave the all-clear, crossing back into the living room area. Pacey wondered if Dawson could protect him, and check their room. Joey hated Pacey mocking her, playing the helpless woman. It was an act that Pacey prided himself on and always gained an obligatory laugh from Dawson.

Soon everyone was giving the place the once-over, looking everywhere with anticipation, and finding, to their relief, nothing. They spent the rest of the evening talking about everything that had happened to them in the short time they'd been there, lamenting their inability to do anything to really help.

Around midnight, everyone finally wandered off to bed. All but Joey. She wasn't sleepy. She sat in the living room, reading a book by the fire, trying to get ahead in English. She was in the middle of *Medea*, actually having a hard time turning the page because what happened next would just be too horrific on a night like this. Any night, really. How could a woman possibly cook her children and feed them to her husband because she was jealous, angry, whatever? Greek tragedy, it was more like a Stephen King novel. She closed the book, then put another log on the fire. It suddenly felt chilly. The log caught instantly, and blazed warmly in her face. Her cheeks felt flushed as she stood looking outside at the house that none of them could save. That was strange. There was candlelight in the window—Isabella Percy's window! Joey blinked, thinking that her mind was playing tricks on her again. But the light stayed on. Then in the reflection in her window she saw Dawson behind her. The expression on his face said he obviously saw the light, too.

"Let's go check it out, Joe," Dawson said, practically out the door. "The light could be our answer."

Flashlight in hand, they were able to make their way into the house through the kitchen. It was strange that no one had locked the door, but then Dawson's parents rarely locked their own house— the benefit of living in a small town. As they made their way up the stairs they turned off their flashlight, and tried to be quiet. To wake anyone now would cause a ruckus over nothing.

The door to Isabella Percy's wing seemed heavier than yesterday, Dawson thought as he pushed it open. It also creaked loudly, which made them both look around to see if anyone had heard what they thought was a noise loud enough to wake the entire house. But it hadn't. They made their way in, and went straight for Isabella's room, stopping at the door.

"So what's the plan, Dawson? You're the man with the plan." Looking at him she realized he didn't have one. "We've got to have a plan. I mean, what if . . . I don't know, but someone obviously is in there."

Dawson handed Joey the flashlight, and grabbed a vase from a nearby table and armed himself with it, heading in.

"Yeah, that makes me feel real safe," Joey said sarcastically as she followed him.

As soon as they entered, their eyes immediately

went to the light. It was quickly disappearing behind the mantel, which obviously hid some sort of secret passageway. Dawson and Joey exchanged a look. So this was how someone was getting around the mansion, causing all the "accidents." The panel slid shut, leaving them in blackness. Joey flipped on the flashlight, and then began pushing on the mantel, hoping to trigger it. Dawson quickly followed her lead. If they could open the mantel, they could finally find who was behind all of the strange occurrences at the mansion, and maybe even save the plantation. They pulled at everything, but nothing seemed to work.

"We're so close, Joe."

"We've tried everything, Dawson. Maybe you should just lean against the mantel like in one of those old movies and it'll just open." Joey leaned against the mantel, totally frustrated, but also kidding. That's when it opened up, a cold dank draft filling the room.

"If I would have known it was that easy . . ." Dawson joked, and gave Joey a here goes nothing look, and went in. Joey followed, not so sure they were doing the right thing. The mantel closed behind them.

If they thought it was dark in Isabella Percy's room yesterday, it was darker now. To make matters worse, their flashlight started to flicker.

"I don't know about this, Dawson. Maybe we should have gotten help."

Dawson could barely see Joey, but from the sound of her voice, he knew she was really scared. As he turned the flashlight back on the wall, it showed no evidence that there was ever a swinging mantel there. Pushing against it, it was as solid as any wall he'd ever felt. Too late. Dawson now turned his attention back to the tunnel ahead of him. The flashlight's beam fell off after only ten feet.

"Come on," Dawson said, "I won't let anything happen to you. I promise. Now let's find who's behind all of this."

A gust of wind whistled through the tunnel and suddenly it was incredibly cold. Chilly and tentative, Dawson set down the vase he had hastily grabbed. Joey clutched Dawson's arm as they began their venture into the unknown. They walked slowly, their flashlight still flickering, casting strange lights on the wall. The images glowed and dimmed in the dark tunnel, looking like something out of a haunted house. Dawson wondered if the flashlight was really helping them. It reflected little light, but on the positive side it managed to make Joey a clinging vine, and as much as he'd never admit it to her, he liked it. To have her close to him, to know that he was responsible for her safety . . . His adrenaline kicked in.

A light was quickly approaching them from around a corner. Dawson flipped off the flashlight, hoping that it hadn't been seen, and they moved to a crevice in the wall. Joey's heart beat fast in her chest. They would either catch who was behind all of this, or be caught, and then . . . She didn't want to think about it. The accidents that had been happening around the plantation made her think that whoever was responsible wouldn't mind killing someone.

Dawson was so close to Joey he could feel her heart beating. Or was that his own? He'd have to tackle whoever was coming, using surprise as his weapon. If not, the thought of something happening to Joey, well . . . that wasn't an option.

The light was now almost on top of them and Dawson steeled himself, waiting for the just the right second . . . *BAM!* Dawson jumped the man who'd been approaching, pinning him down, sitting on his back, pushing his face against the cold ground.

Joey was the first to see the man's face, gasping in surprise. "Tom Griffin?"

Dawson twisted Tom's arm higher behind his back, as he got him onto his feet, slamming him into the wall. "It's good you like the dark and dank, because you're going to be spending some serious time in jail, Griffin."

"No. Stop," a small voice pleaded. They turned around to see Monique. "He's my boyfriend."

"He's your *what*?" Joey was really confused.

"Despite what Uncle Winston said, Tom didn't steal anything. I gave the locket to him to wear for safe-keeping. He's helping me try to save my home. You see, the locket I lost belonged to my great, great, great, great, great, great aunt Isabella Percy. It has a secret compartment." Monique demonstrated the locket opening normally, and then she pushed where the chain met the locket and a secret compartment popped out from under the picture of her ancestor. "It's a map that obviously belonged to John Sheridan."

Joey took it carefully in her hand and unfolded it. It was old, and yellowed. And as Joey shone her flashlight at the paper, she could see many lines, leading here and there, and despite a hole in the map, it obviously led to a treasure.

Dawson let go of Tom, apologizing, "I'm sorry, man."

Tom smiled, telling them that with the treasure they could save the Percy Plantation. The only problem being . . . Tom pointed to the hole in the map.

"It's not that big a hole. It can't take that long to explore," Dawson commented. "Let us help you."

Monique and Tom exchanged a look. They were covered in grime, and help could only accelerate the process. The hole in the map had been a bigger obstacle to John Sheridan's treasure than they had calculated.

"I'd really like that," Monique said, hugging Joey. Tom shook Dawson's hand, happy to have someone on their side. "And obviously you can't tell Uncle Winston. Where Tom's concerned he can't see straight."

"We'll tell him after we find the treasure. Then everything will be okay," Tom said, putting his arm around Monique. He obviously loved her. That was plain for Dawson and Joey to see.

14

Vision of Blood Dancing in My Head

Pacey woke with a start, sitting straight up. He wasn't having a nightmare, so why was he awake? Had someone made a noise? He rubbed his head, confused. Jack snored from the sofa, but the twin bed next to him was empty. Where was Dawson? He walked out into the living room and saw a flashlight beam making its way toward the bayou. Pacey could make out two figures behind the flashlight. Could it be Dawson, and . . . Pacey looked in the girls' room. Joey was gone, too. Where could they be going?

He quickly threw on some jeans and a T-shirt, hopping out the door as he forced on his tennis shoes. Without a flashlight he was stumbling in the dark. There was no light anywhere now; clouds were covering whatever moonlight had been in the sky. Pacey trudged forward, expecting to find Dawson and Joey just ahead. Instead he found himself in the middle of the bayou, his sneakers now covered in mud, and sinking with every step he took.

"Well, this was smart. If this was an episode of *Gilligan's Island,* I'd be up to my neck in quicksand right now," Pacey said to the night. Just then he heard a small splash. He could see something moving toward him. Something in the water. This obviously wasn't good.

He quickly backpedaled, trying to find his way out of the mush. The clouds cleared, giving him a small ounce of light. Enough light to see that it was a gator approaching.

"Please be Le Beau? No, that's *Hogan's Heroes.* Think, think, what's his name? It's a foo-foo name . . . When I close my eyes I picture annoying crab . . . Sebastian?" Now instead of talking to himself, he looked at the alligator. "Sebastian? Sebastian? It's you, right?" The gator stopped. "See, I remember your name. Which means we're friends, and friends don't cannibalize other friends—unless of course you're the Donner Party. Now Monique would have fed you dinner, right? Maybe a chicken or a cow. Something filling. So we should be cool." The gator started toward him again. "But you're a big boy, so still hungry, right?" Pacey quickly rummaged through his pockets. An old movie stub, his lucky penny that didn't feel too lucky at the moment . . . Lifesavers. "It's food, right? One of the five food groups, possibly qualifying as a fruit." The gator

opened its mouth. "And you obviously want one."
Pacey threw in a few Lifesavers. Sebastian closed his
mouth, and if Pacey didn't know better he thought
he saw a smile. Of course, a gator's got a lot of teeth.

"I like the red ones, too. You know, that look is
good for you. Mouth closed. Not so threatening."
Pacey popped a Lifesaver. "So, you have any idea
where they went?"

The alligator looked at him like he was crazy, then
crept closer, butting him with its head.

"Hey, I just said you were nice. Don't make me
take that back."

The alligator nudged him again. If Pacey didn't
know better he'd think that the alligator wanted to
be petted. It was bizarre. He bent down hesitantly
and put his hand out, wondering if it'd get bitten off.
Miraculously it wasn't. And he began patting the
gator on the head.

"You definitely need lotion. Not going to get any
babes with skin like that." The gator looked up at
him as if offended, and backed away, heading toward
the water.

"Hey wait! I didn't mean anything by that." The
gator stopped, looked at him with its big glassy eyes.

"You actually are like a dog. Not cuddly or anything, but on the intelligent side. Now, you've been
out here all night long. You know what's been goin'
down, so I think you really can help me find my
friends. Joey and Dawson. Dawson's blond, about
this tall, and you know what? Describing guys, not
so fun. Now Joey, you'd remember her. Brunette,
with soft brown eyes, that can look right into you.

Melt your heart. You know the kind. Your owner actually falls into that category—different color eyes, but same general principle." Pacey threw the gator another Lifesaver. Snap! He caught it, his jaw making a horrible sound. "Okay, maybe no tossing. Not so fond of that noise. As nice as you are, that noise gives me the heebie-jeebies." Pacey actually began to relax. Maybe Monique was right. Maybe Sebastian didn't eat people.

Pacey looked around, trying to get his bearings. The only reason he'd come out here was to find Joey and Dawson. Where were they? He knew the mansion was behind him, staring off into the dark, trying to see its outline. He'd walked so long he wasn't sure what direction he was facing. He closed his eyes for a moment. That's when it hit! His head ached so badly he almost fell to the ground. Behind his eyelids lightning flashed. Then the vision came.

A small tin box.

Old.

Worn.

And then the box began to beat like a heart. The beating got louder and louder until it was almost deafening. In his mind he tried to pry open the box, anything to stop the noise. The more he tried, the faster the beating became. Blood began to ooze from the sides of the box. He dropped the box. It didn't fall, but floated in space like a small coffin. And then it finally opened, on its own, blood flowing from it like a river.

Physically Pacey backed away. Though his eyes were now open, he could only see his vision.

The gator sank back into the bayou.

Pacey continued to back away, falling against the bank of the bayou, into the cold green moss that covered it. He sat there for a minute, hands to his eyes, willing the world to be normal again.

No more blood.

No more box.

No more visions.

A wave of nausea overcame him, and he began to heave. *When would this stop?* It was scaring the hell out of him. *And what did it all mean?*

15

What About Love?

Dawson and Joey spent a good forty-five minutes exploring the tunnels with Tom and Monique. The couple said that they'd been looking through the tunnels for three weeks now, and there still seemed to be a thousand different twists and turns. They were grateful to have help, despite the fact that they had wanted to keep their discovery a secret.

The kids from Capeside had recovered from their earlier qualms and were now enjoying the mystique of the tunnels . . . knowing that there was no one else to run into. Dawson began to appreciate the Indiana Jones aspect of the scenario, and he noticed that Joey was peering into the nooks and crannies of the tunnels with deep fascination. He nudged her. "Turned out to be not so bad, hmm?"

Joey smiled at him in the dark. "Yeah, thank God. It's going to be so weird . . . we can't tell anyone about this."

Monique turned around. "Yes, please don't. Even Jen. I mean, I want to tell everyone eventually, but the reason I'm not telling Uncle Winston—"

"Aside from the fact that he's convinced I'm behind all the sabotage that's been going on here—" Tom interrupted.

Monique smiled. "Yes, aside from that, is because I don't want Uncle Winston to get his hopes up, you know? It's our last chance, and even this . . . well, this is pretty farfetched."

"Don't think that way," Dawson said, comforting her. Monique smiled her thanks in return.

Monique dusted the debris from the tunnel off of her shirt, whipping her hair back up into a neat ponytail. She didn't want to run into Uncle Winston in the hallway with the remnants of the tunnel still on her clothing.

"You guys," she whispered. "We should get back into the house. Uncle Winston's taken to making late night rounds ever since weird things started happening around the plantation. I think he's afraid I'm going to get abducted in my sleep or something."

"Or worse—I might show up in the dead of the night," Tom said, widening his eyes and wiggling his fingers teasingly at Monique. Monique laughed.

"God forbid," Monique said. "Let's get out of here. There's a chill tonight. Do you have the map?" she asked Tom.

"I hope so," Dawson said. "I don't think I'd be able to find my way back into the house by myself."

Joey smiled at this. "Come on, how many different ways can there be to go underground?"

"Oh, you'd be amazed," Monique said. "Some of the paths stretch for over a mile. It can get pretty scary if you take a wrong turn. I've gotten panicked myself more than once."

"Which is why we don't go in alone anymore," Tom said. Monique nodded in agreement.

Joey looked around the cold, damp walls of the tunnel. What if you were caught in these tunnels and your lantern went out? She couldn't imagine how terrifying it would have been to run into someone else in these tunnels. Suddenly, the pieces of the story behind this plantation started to make more sense to her. Clearly, there was a lot more to it than was obvious on the surface. Now that she was underground, experiencing these tunnels, she could get a glimpse of what the plantation must have been like when John and Isabella lived there. Sneaking through these tunnels with the war going on around them . . . the ground must have been shaking from the gunshots and cannons. They must have been afraid. She looked at Dawson, in awe for a moment that he could have appreciated this aspect of history before he even saw these tunnels. She still wasn't on board with the entire romantic picture he had painted, but it was beginning to sink in that she had definitely stepped into a poignant piece of history.

That night, when they had seen Tom, Joey had thought for a moment that she and Dawson were about to be killed. She had been thrown for a loop

discovering that Tom and Monique were dating. She
had long been convinced that Tom was the bad guy,
though she hadn't made that opinion entirely public.
Now she had to retrace her steps in order to rethink
her reasoning. How many enemies could this sweet
girl possibly have? Joey found herself wondering if
maybe it wasn't an enemy after all . . . at least not
something of flesh and blood. She shuddered, pushing the thoughts out of her mind. Crawling around
in a dark abandoned tunnel was not a good time to
turn one's thoughts to the otherworldly.

Joey and Dawson were following Tom and Monique
out of the winding tunnels. They had agreed that they
were saving the final tunnel for tomorrow night, the
night of the ball. Monique said that it was the most
intricate tunnel, so it would be good for them to go
through it during the party, when there was too much
chaos to notice the missing kids.

"You don't want to miss the whole ball, though, do
you?" Joey asked Monique.

Monique shrugged. "I don't know. It's going to be
strange to be there without my parents. And to tell
you the truth, I don't know how many people are
even going to show up."

"Why do you say that?" Dawson asked.

"Because," Monique explained. "People in town
have heard that the bank might foreclose. There's
nothing people like better than to see a good name
be ruined."

"Do you really think so?" Dawson said, incredulous. Joey snorted. How could Dawson even ask
that, knowing what she had been through? People in

Capeside were always all ears when it came to the Potter family, despite the fact that it was clearly none of their business.

"I really think so," Monique said. "I mean, I don't exactly want to be here, either, not at the moment. Still, this is my home. It's where I grew up, where my parents lived. Aside from my own memories, it's all I've got left of them. I've got to stay to save it, no matter what. Besides, even if I wanted to attempt to enjoy the ball, we've still got to look through the tunnel tomorrow. The bank is threatening to foreclose the day after—we won't have enough time if we wait."

The words sounded so familiar to Joey she almost felt as if she'd been hit in the stomach. It reminded her of her own past, desperately trying to save her home and the Potter B&B. She would have spoken up, but it seemed inappropriate to say something to Monique, especially when the Bed and Breakfast was flourishing now. Joey shivered in the damp tunnel, feeling bad for Monique. Joey knew what it was to sacrifice for your family, but it would be awful to be trapped on this sprawling plantation, with its dark, locked chambers and cold, hidden tunnels. Tom and Monique were slightly ahead of Joey and Dawson now. Joey looked up at Dawson. It was strange, but he seemed to be enjoying himself.

She shined her flashlight in his face. "What are you all smiley about?"

"I'm not smiley," Dawson said. But he smiled.

"Clearly, you are," Joey said.

"Well, come on, Joe, isn't this cool?" Dawson asked her.

"It's cool that Tom didn't turn out to be an evil guy who was trying to steal from this family, but aside from that . . . no. This is still pretty creepy, Dawson. Not cool. We could have been killed in here."

Dawson rolled his eyes. He knew that they weren't meant to die here. Not that Dawson could claim that he was any sort of psychic, but he knew when he had a bad feeling about something. He didn't have a bad feeling about this. No, he had a feeling of adventure, intrigue. And these tunnels were amazing! He reached over and took the flashlight from Joey's hand. Tom had given them extra batteries, so Dawson washed the beam of light over the walls of the tunnels so he could finally see what they looked like.

"Look at it in here. Can you believe that this network of tunnels exists under the house we've been staying in? That Jen came to visit as a child? John and Isabella probably came to rendezvous down here," Dawson speculated.

"You make them sound like soap opera characters." Joey smiled.

"They are, in a way," Dawson replied. "Think of it, Joey. The secret affair they must have had, the danger of the war around them . . ."

"Yeah, it's really romantic to think about Yankees coming, killing your lover and stealing your gold," Joey countered.

"Maybe they didn't steal it," Dawson offered.

"Yes, and maybe John and Isabella lived happily ever after. Come on, Dawson."

Dawson started to laugh for real now. You could

take Joey Potter thousands of miles away, plunk her down in a strange town, in a creepy plantation, and she would still find a way to work her cynicism into any situation. At least she was consistent.

"Joey, you know as well as I do that there's no way of knowing what happened. But their love sounded pretty pure. He probably saved her life. Think about it. He was based on this plantation to guard not only the land, but also the love of his life. You don't find that to be at all romantic? I mean, you'd be the first to say there are few men who would do that."

Joey was getting angry, and didn't particularly feel like playing out this repetitive argument, particularly in a dank tunnel. Dawson knew her better than anyone. Then why was he acting as if her opinions were so one-sided? She had already started to feel compassion for John and Isabella, now that she was in these tunnels. But did she have to make them into romantic superheroes? It wasn't that she didn't believe in the power of love. She did. Joey just wasn't sure she believed that love was so powerful it could survive one of the bloodiest wars in history. And she didn't particularly feel like speculating on the character of a man she didn't know.

"Dawson, you're starting to put words in my mouth. It's like you enjoy bickering with me, which is funny, since you know the outcome."

"I don't enjoy arguing with you, Joe. Okay, maybe there is a certain pleasure. Look, I guess I'm just trying to get to the bottom of why you're so set against the story of this couple," Dawson said. He stopped walking for a moment. Tom and Monique were getting farther and farther ahead of them, but Dawson stood still, in the dark, trying to get Joey to look him in the eye.

Joey was confused, and now that Monique and Tom were so far ahead, she was getting nervous again. "I'm not against their story, Dawson," she said. "I'm just against creating a story for them when we don't know what happened. I mean, if you wanna know what I really think, I think you're just manipulating what their affair was like for your own personal gain. Like you're trying to get through to me."

"Well, maybe I am!" Dawson said. "Maybe I wonder why you're so bitter about love when you've had such great love offered to you."

That comment made both of them fall into silence. Joey and Dawson stood there for a moment, staring at each other, the flashlight illuminating them. Joey hardly knew what to say. She knew what Dawson was getting at, and she didn't know how to explain what she meant, or how she felt.

"Look, Dawson . . . I know what you're saying, and I know that it's true. I guess all I mean is that you can't know the ins and outs of somebody's relationship, or even the ins and outs of somebody's heart, unless you are that person, or unless you've been in that relationship. And I know that things don't always work out. So maybe that's made me be careful. And you can call me crazy, and try to convince me to go blindly forth into the world like you, but I don't think it's such a bad thing to be careful of your heart." She paused for a moment, breathless, wondering why on earth she was choosing this moment, in this godforsaken tunnel, to be so honest.

Dawson and Joey walked in silence, thoughtful, until they met up with Tom and Monique at the tunnel's entrance into the house. The four discussed their plan to meet the next evening during the ball. Tom said that he would be at the masquerade, safely in disguise, and that he would come get Dawson and Joey when they were ready to go to the tunnel. Everyone was excited about the adventure that was ahead of them, and of the possibility of saving the plantation for Monique and her uncle. However, despite their excitement and relief, Dawson and Joey were obviously a little "off." They shifted beside each other as Tom and Monique planned the next evening, and they could feel the tension in the air between them. Joey was wondering what she was so upset about. Sometimes she wondered if she was fighting with Dawson just to fight with him, because agreeing with him might mean something different. Something she wasn't ready to stir up again. She thought for a split second of turning to Dawson and admitting as much, just to finally clear the air between them, but it didn't seem like the right time. But what were they even fighting about? Were they really up in arms about the romance factor between a Confederate soldier and his lover? Or were they up in arms about the romance factor between the two of them?

Tom leaned in and kissed Monique good night—a

long, sweet kiss. Joey felt bad for a moment that the two of them had to sneak around, when Monique was obviously so smitten with Tom. However, just as Joey was starting to soften, Dawson leaned in and whispered, "See? Even in the most dire situation, love seems to prevail."

Joey, annoyed, tapped Dawson on the chest. "Gimmee a break," she muttered. Monique wrinkled her forehead at the two of them, wondering what was going on. Tom groped along the wall of the tunnel, searching for a crevice. There were four notches, Dawson saw, in the hidden door. Tom pressed the third notch down, and the door clicked, swinging open. The four teenagers quietly open the door of the tunnel, creeping back into the pitch-black room on the other side. In the dark, Joey reached out and grabbed onto Dawson's arm, tip-toeing behind him out into the hallway. Dawson looked back at her as she touched his arm, but didn't say anything. Whatever was going on between the two of them, they seemed to have silently declared a truce. The four bid each other a silent good night by the stairwell, then slipped off into the darkness, their minds racing with thoughts of what was to come.

16

The Man in the Mask

The next night, the kids almost forgot all the chaos at the plantation. It was impossible not to get caught up in the romance of the spectacular masquerade ball. Dawson and Joey walked into the mansion from the guesthouse first and the view took their breath away.

"Wow," Joey breathed. "With everything that's going on at this place, I can't believe they pulled this off."

Dawson nodded in agreement. He wondered who had come in the middle of the night to create this wonderland; it hardly seemed like the struggling plantation had enough employees at the moment to pull off this sort of gorgeous spectacle. Dawson smiled to himself. Maybe it was Elolie's good voodoo

179

magic at work. Perhaps she had blessed herself with the power to stay up through the night and work through the day to throw what looked like the most amazing party Dawson and Joey had ever attended. Of course, their partygoing history wasn't that fantastic, so that wasn't really saying much.

Dawson glanced at Joey, who was tasteful and elegant as per usual in a strapless black gown, no jewelry aside from her mother's bracelet, and her hair swept up with tendrils curling down the side of her face. He couldn't believe that Joey was so utterly unaware of her striking beauty. In fact, she was probably glad that she got to hide behind the elaborate mask Monique had provided her with for the evening. Dawson knew she would feel uncomfortable if she caught him gazing at her, so he quickly redirected his attention back to the main foyer of the house.

The entrance to the house was lined with magnolia boughs, as were many of the walls and other doorways. Every room was fragrant and touched by the soft, white glow provided by not only the gorgeous flowers but also by the twinkling white lights strung along the woodwork.

Monique, Jen, and Jack came in behind Dawson and Joey. They were also dressed to the nines, though their faces were obscured. Joey grinned at them, lifting her mask for a moment.

"Suddenly I feel like we're in a bizarro version of *Eyes Wide Shut*," Joey laughed.

Monique groaned. "Don't say that. We've got enough trouble on our hands." Then Monique smiled. She was excited tonight, and only Dawson and Joey knew the real reason. She was determined not to let her worries about the plantation get the better of her tonight, not when she knew she was going to be able to save it.

Monique reached over and touched Jen's arm. "Hey," she said. "Let's go watch people arrive up at the second floor landing. It's the best part of the night."

Excited, Jen, Jack, Joey, and Dawson followed Monique up the stairs. Pacey and Andie had already gone into the ballroom, caught up with the thrill of the crowd. From the second floor landing, outside of Isabella Percy's wing, they had a clear view of masked, gorgeously outfitted couples entering the residence and sweeping around the ballroom. If they had thought the ballroom was spectacular when they first arrived at the plantation, their awe had now increased tenfold. The chandelier had been replaced and filled the massive ballroom with a golden glow. It was true that everyone looked better by candle-light. The room wasn't dim by any means, but the light cast by the hundreds of candles in the grand chandelier, as well as the white lights lining the walls, made the guests at the Percy Masquerade Ball look as if they were from another era. Obviously, their costumes were part of that.

"I might be jaded," Joey said, shaking her head, "but those people look amazing."

"Well, so do you guys." Monique smiled. "I'm so glad we had enough masks to go around."

Dawson agreed. "It looks like something from

Labyrinth. You know, that scene where Jennifer Connolly arrives at the ball and David Bowie swoops in to dance with her . . ." Joey rolled her eyes at Dawson's movie references, but she had to admit it was true. It was like a fairy tale. Watching the guests arrive and seeing them promenade around the ballroom was more beautiful than anything she might have imagined.

Monique sighed. "You know, this is where Isabella used to watch for John. I think it's where she first saw him—the night of the ball, where they met."

"Well, that's a romantic notion," Dawson said pointedly, looking at Joey. Joey looked back at him and rolled her eyes. Then she wrinkled her forehead, scrunching up her nose.

"Do you guys smell that?" Joey asked. Everyone paused for a moment, sniffing the air.

"Smoke," Jack said.

"Exactly," said Joey. Without another word, the four kids bolted toward the source of the smoke. To their horror, it seemed to be coming from the South Wing!

Monique arrived first at the forbidden door that led into Isabella Percy's wing. Before she barreled through the door, Dawson grabbed her arm and said urgently, "Wait—check to see if it's hot first." He placed his hand on the metal knob to see if it was hot to the touch. Fortunately, it wasn't and the gang proceeded to venture gently into the wing.

It was dark, as per usual, only now the South Wing was murky with a thin layer of smoke. The tinkling glasses and muted laughter from the ballroom now seemed a million miles away as the kids plunged into the darkness of Isabella's former residence. Dawson was ahead of the others, reaching his arms tentatively into the darkness. He saw through the dimly filtered light where the smoke was coming from; long muslin curtains were burning in Isabella's former study!

Dawson moved forward, indicating that the others should hang back for a second. He didn't want all of them getting struck with smoke inhalation. As Dawson came closer to the flames licking at the old, dusty drapery, he noticed that there was a small shrine on the window seat. It looked like a bundle of bones, with lace tied around it, scattered with burnt petals. Dawson wondered fleetingly if perhaps the lace was from Isabella's dresses. Could she really be behind all of this?

Dawson turned and gathered up the small rug on the floor behind him and began swatting the flames firmly with it, beginning to quell the fire. Just then, Dawson heard footsteps pounding on the floor behind him. He whirled around and peered through the darkness, just in time to see the shadowy figure of a masked man in a black cape sprinting by!

"Hey! You! Stop!" Dawson bellowed. He dropped the rug, looking anxiously at the flames. He didn't want the fire to worsen, but he also didn't want the culprit to get away. He moved toward the masked man, who barreled into Joey and nearly knocked over Monique, Jen, and Jack as he ran past them. Jack reached after the man and tried to grasp onto his cape, but he was too late.

Dawson ran to Joey, breathless. "Are you okay?"

Joey nodded. "Yeah, I think he just knocked out a rib or two," she said. "Listen, you guys put out the fire before it gets worse. We'll go down and see if we can find that creep."

Monique's face was crestfallen. This was obviously not what she had planned for the evening—more harm to her home. "Trying to find a masked man at a masquerade ball? That's going to be like finding a needle in a haystack."

Jen put her hand on her cousin's shoulder. "Come on, sweetie, let's not give up so soon."

"After all, not all of those men will be covered in soot," Jack offered.

Monique almost smiled at that as she, Jen, and Joey took off after the masked man. Jack fell in with Dawson in the study, slamming the rug against the flaming curtains. It wasn't difficult to put the fire out, but the two of them wondered just how bad it would have gotten if they hadn't been hovering outside of the South Wing.

"I guess we shouldn't obsess about what could have gone wrong too much at this point," Jack said. He and Dawson were feeling along the window seat and what remained of the curtains, making sure there were no more burning embers that could erupt into fire.

"Yeah, that could just snowball and lead us into a full-blown freak-out," Dawson said. He fell into silence then, thinking about what the rest of the evening held. He wondered if this would interfere with their plans to go back into the tunnels tonight. And whoever this man was . . . did he know about the tunnels? Did he know about the gold? What if he had already gotten in there? Suddenly, Dawson had visions of Indiana Jones dancing in his head. Getting trapped in those tunnels with a dangerous stranger . . . that would certainly be at the top of the list of very bad things. But Dawson had to wonder if it was indeed a stranger. It would be someone who knew the house, who knew that Isabella's wing was sacred, who knew when people would or wouldn't be in the house. Maybe even someone who was interested in the house for his own purposes . . . and worse, interested in Monique. Dawson snapped himself out of his thought pattern as he realized he and Jack were standing alone in the dark and forbidden wing of Isabella Percy when they should probably be catching up with the others.

Jen, Joey, and Monique ran down the stairs. Their masks were resting on top of their heads, and they had their skirts gathered up in their arms to keep from tripping.

"Man," Jen muttered. "Formal wear is so not good for catching a criminal."

"Well, if Charlie's Angels can do it, so can we." Joey said.

"Only they probably just ripped off their dresses at this point," Monique said.

"If only I'd worn my leather body suit underneath this!" Jen joked.

However, it didn't really seem like an appropriate time to be joking. When the three girls arrived at the main ballroom, their faces fell in dismay.

Hundreds of guests had arrived since they'd left their post at the second-floor landing. The ballroom

was a throng of costumed people, and all their elaborate masks were blending together. To top it off, it
had obviously been dark and smoke-filled in Isabella's wing; they hadn't even gotten that good of a
look at the masked man's actual mask.

Joey looked at Monique and took a deep breath.
She knew all the thoughts that were probably running through Monique's head tonight. Now that Joey
knew more about what was going on, she desperately wanted to help Monique. But what if this man
running through the crowds tried to do something to
further harm Monique's home, or worse, Monique
herself?

"Maybe we should split up," Joey said. "And just
try to cover as much ground as we can before he gets
too far. Does everyone vaguely remember what the
guy looked like?"

The other two girls nodded in silence. No one
wanted to admit just how vague their recollections
were.

17

Hitting the Dance Floor

Joey made her way across the dance floor. She now had her mask back on her face, which gave her the feeling that she was moving in a dream, sifting through a cast of bizarre characters. It also made her feel protected, somehow, to be in disguise. If she could recognize the masked man, she was sure he would be able to recognize her. She wondered if he would try something to harm her, since he knew that she was a witness to the crime.

She couldn't believe how many people were on this dance floor. All these members of high society were completely oblivious that the estate was crumbling beneath their feet because someone wanted to destroy this family. Or maybe some of them weren't oblivious. Joey's eyes narrowed. As Joey brushed through the guests of the masquerade, smelling their expensive perfume, she was reminded of members of the Yacht Club and Country Club back in Capeside. Joey felt like those people were the same no matter where you went. Despite the fact that Joey didn't want to make such sweeping generalizations, she couldn't help but draw on her own past experiences. She wondered for a moment if the reason this party had gotten so crowded was simply to see if the Percys would meet their downfall tonight. Joey remembered what Monique had said in the tunnel. After all, someone was definitely out to get this family, and there was no better entertainment for a town of blue bloods than seeing a good family lose its fortune.

Joey shook her head. She was letting her thoughts run away with her, when really she should be concentrating on finding the masked man. She looked deep into the crowd, trying to focus. Suddenly, she caught a glimpse of a mask that seemed familiar. A tall man in black was wearing the mask, which had crushed velvet sweeping away from the eyes, and the nose of a hawk. Joey thought that this was the mask she had seen up in the study. She watched the man move through the crowd for a moment. Creep. He was so nonchalant, thinking he could get away with a crime and then just roam around the dance floor. Joey fixed her gaze on him and moved slowly through the crowd, following the stranger.

Her heart was racing. She didn't see her friends anywhere, and despite the fact that she was a guest in this house, she felt as if she were suddenly in the middle of nowhere. Hiding behind her mask, Joey didn't even feel like herself. She felt daring. And she felt certain that she was just about to catch the man who was trying to sabotage the Percys' well-being.

She was inches away from the stranger. He wasn't wearing his cape anymore, but she was sure it was him. He was the same height, and now that she was close, she knew for sure she'd seen that mask before. Before she could talk herself out of it, Joey lunged forward, grabbing the stranger firmly by the shoulder and reaching to rip off his mask.

The man whirled around, his arms up in defense. "Hey!" he yelled, struggling to keep the mask on his face. But Joey was determined, and she wrenched the elastic over the stranger's face, eager to see who the man was behind the mayhem.

The man was Pacey! Joey and Pacey stared at each other for a moment, breathless. Then Pacey cracked a smile. He could see Joey was upset, maybe even scared. He took her by the shoulders, hugging her.

"Hey, kiddo. What was that all about? It's just me," Pacey said.

Joey shook her head sadly. "I know. God, I'm such an idiot. It's a long story . . ."

She relayed to Pacey that she and Dawson and the others had discovered the fire in the South Wing, and that they were now searching for the man in the mask.

"But if your mask looks just like his, there's a good chance that one out of every ten men in the house is wearing the same exact thing," Joey sighed. She gazed out on the chaos of the ballroom, black masks swimming in front of her eyes.

"It's okay," Pacey said gently. "Look, with all of us looking for this guy, we're bound to find him. And we'll stick together with this. We should find Andie. This is like a dream come true for her."

Joey smiled. Pacey knew how to relax her and get her to focus. And he was right; Andie would be all over solving the case.

Jen and Monique approached the dancing couple. Monique seemed to be quite upset. She gave Joey a pointed look, and Joey knew exactly what Monique was thinking: *What was going on? They didn't have time for this. They needed to search the last tunnels.*

"Any sign?" Jen asked.

"Not yet," Joey said sadly.

"We'll get him," Monique said. She set her jaw, determined, and peered out into the crowd. "The scary thing," she mused, "is that I know everyone in this house tonight, in one way or another. Who would do this to someone they knew?" No sooner were the words out of Monique's mouth than she spotted someone across the room. Her eyes narrowed.

"What? What is it?" Jen asked. She followed Monique's gaze and let out a sigh as she recognized who Monique was glaring at.

Michael Stetcher. He was dashing in a tailored tuxedo, but his mask was resting on the back of his head, so they weren't sure if it was the mask they were looking for. Still, Monique obviously didn't feel the need to check and see if the clues stacked up; she seemed convinced that Michael Stetcher was the man, and she was apparently marching across the ballroom to tell him so.

"Oh, man . . ." Jen said as Monique stormed off. "I'd better chaperone this one."

As Jen followed Monique, Joey turned to Pacey. "Do you really think it's him?"

Pacey shrugged. "Man, at this point, anything is possible. I hope not. I mean, he seemed like a nice guy, right?"

Joey shook her head, uncertain. "I don't know," she pondered. "Sure, he seems nice, but I don't know why he's advising Monique to sell the place when he knows she doesn't want to. Seems a little suspicious."

Meanwhile, Monique was face to unmasked face with Michael Stetcher, and she was fuming. Jen stood warily behind her cousin.

"It was you, wasn't it?" Monique demanded.

Michael looked at Monique as if she were crazy. "Monique, what is wrong with you?"

Monique had had enough of small talk. She straightened up and locked eyes with Michael. "Someone, a masked man, set a small fire in Isabella's wing tonight. If we hadn't been upstairs at the time it could have destroyed the entire wing, and spread to the rest of the house. This house, Michael. My parents' house."

Michael's eyes widened, and he put his hand on Monique's shoulder. "Are you serious?" he asked. "Why didn't you tell me right away? Are you okay?"

"Michael," Monique said firmly. "Don't you find it interesting that someone might attempt an attack on my home at the very same party attended by a certain gentlemen who was trying to convince me to *sell* my home?"

Michael was appalled. He didn't look as if he even knew what to say in response to Monique's accusations. "Monique," he said quietly. "I fail to see what one thing has to do with the other."

"Because!" Monique cried. "You've been advising me to sell for months now, and you know I don't want to do that. In fact, you know I would never do that!"

"I've been advising you to do that because I really think it would be the best thing, Monique. There are no ulterior motives, here. You and Winston don't have the means—"

Monique squeezed her eyes shut. "Don't give me this song and dance again, Michael! Don't stomp out miracles before they happen. I have plans in mind. This could work. We could come through at the last minute and pay off the—"

But before Monique could finish her sentence, a distinguished older gentleman danced by with a woman. He stopped in his waltz and slapped Michael on the back. "Making plans for the property, son?"

Michael glanced at Monique, appalled by the man who was obviously his father. But it was too late. Mr. Stetcher had already done the damage and was apparently unaware of the present tension. He turned his gaze to Monique.

"Beautiful party, honey. A nice way to say goodbye to the place," Mr. Stetcher said. With a wide grin, the man danced away, leaving Monique to stare at Michael in horror.

Michael touched Monique's arm again, gently.

"Monique, I'm sorry, but you're not going to get your last-minute miracle. I'm just trying to be realistic, and in doing so, I'm trying to protect you."

Monique wasn't having it, however. She stepped away from Michael, brushing off his arm. "Protect me? You can say what you like, Michael, but the only reason I can think of why you would be so set on me selling this house is because of some devious motive you have. Why else would you try to sell me so hard on something that I was so clearly set against? And seeing as you know how stubborn I am, looks like there was nothing better for you to do than to try to drive me out with a fire. Were you responsible for the rest, too?"

Michael was clearly getting frustrated now. He turned to Jen. "Jen, you know me. You've known me for years. Would I do this?"

"Don't get me into this, Michael. I'm just trying to help Monique figure out who's behind this," Jen said. She took Monique's hand, squeezing it.

"It's not me," Michael insisted.

"Well, as of right now, you're the only suspect," Monique said. "The only reason I'm not calling the police right now is because I obviously don't have hard evidence. But you're the only one with a motive, Michael. We may have history, but at the same time, it doesn't mean you haven't used that history to your advantage. Right now, I'd believe anything. I mean, you stood here and acted like you weren't trying to manipulate me. Meanwhile, you seem to have discussed floor plans with your father. I don't really see the remorse, Michael."

And with that, Monique turned on her heel and walked away, taking Jen with her. Michael stood there, staring after the girls blankly, a solitary figure in a room full of dancing masks.

Meanwhile, Pacey and Joey were still musing on how Andie would save the day with her years of Nancy Drew reading under her belt. They were just about to search the ballroom for the girl they knew would be able to organize their little S.W.A.T. team into action. However, Dawson had beaten them to the punch. He appeared, breaking through a cluster of people, with Andie by his side. They came up close to Joey and Pacey and whispered conspiratorially.

"Okay, I filled Andie in," Dawson whispered.

Joey stifled a giggle. "Dawson, you don't have to whisper. You're already wearing a mask."

"This would be sooo cool if it weren't already so creepy," Andie said excitedly. "We are gonna get that guy and we are going to kick his butt!"

"Okay, simmer down there, Nancy Drew. We don't want to draw attention to ourselves," Pacey said.

"Of course not," Andie replied. "But we wanna find this guy, right? So here's what we do . . ."

Dawson blocked Andie out for a moment. He had already heard Andie's plan, so he let her words wash over him like water while he concentrated on his own thoughts. They wanted to be inconspicuous, so they were going to pair up and dance around the ballroom, all the while searching for the suspect. They figured that this would be a better plan than standing as a group in the center of the ballroom, staring at people, wide-eyed and suspicious.

Dawson was worried about how this evening was going to pan out. He had originally thought that exploring the final tunnel with Tom and Monique was going to be fairly simple, though it would also obviously be an adventure. He supposed he had been in denial of just how much danger was hanging over them. They weren't in Capeside anymore. Dawson hated the fact that someone, something, was after them and he was helpless to control it. If this man had started a fire in a remote wing of the house, the level of his crimes would only get higher. Dawson feared the worst.

The gang had scattered and split off into couples. Jack and Andie were dancing together, all the while craning their necks, looking for the masked man.

"This feels like an old episode of *Moonlighting*," Andie said.

Jack laughed. "You've been watching way too much Bravo Network. Besides, Bruce Willis and Cybil Shepard weren't pathetic brother and sister like we are."

"Pathetic!" Andie said. "I resent that. We could do a lot worse. You clean up real nice, and so do I, I might add."

Jack smiled. "Yeah, yeah. It's just funny that we always end up with each other. Not that I thought I was going to find love in New Orleans this week or anything . . ."

"Oh, sure you did," Andie joked. "Part of you thought that maybe Danny from *The Real World* would still be down here."

"No, no," Jack laughed. "But I mean, here we are at this crazy romantic ball, dancing with each other. It just gets to me sometimes."

Andie nodded in silence. It got to her, also, but she didn't want to bring Jack down.

"Well, I love you, Jack. Even if you're the most depressing brother ever. I guess it's a good thing that we're not even here to have a good time anymore. We're here to find that man."

Jack nodded, smiling at his sensible sister. Just then, he felt someone tap his shoulder. Jack turned around quickly. He was still jumpy; he had been since he got out of the car and first set eyes on the Percy Plantation. But the masked gentleman who had come up behind him was none other than Pacey.

"Hey, Pace. What's up? Did you find the culprit and now we can all relax?"

Pacey shook his head. "Not so much, no. I was just hoping to dance with your sister."

"Oh, I see how it is," Jack laughed. "You cut in with Andie and I go wander the dance floor alone, certain to be kidnapped by a masked man, dragged into the bayou and left for dead?"

"Yeah, something like that," Pacey said. He knocked Jack playfully on the shoulder as Jack walked away.

"Hey, beautiful." Pacey said to Andie. Andie did look great. All of them, in fact, looked completely different than they did when they were just knocking around Capeside. It wasn't just the fancy clothing and the elaborate masks. The danger and adventure had given them all a flushed, vibrant look to their faces.

"Hey, yourself. You gonna talk to me about what's going on? "Andie said. She could still read Pacey like a book, just as much as she still loved dancing with him.

"Oh, I don't know. Maybe it's this whole notion of, you know, the plantation being under sabotage, our lives being in danger . . ."

Andie rolled her eyes. "Yeah, yeah, I know. But I'm talking about you, Pacey. Come on, I know you're a rock under pressure. Something else is bothering you."

Pacey hesitated. Obviously, he knew he could trust Andie with anything. Still, he hadn't really admitted to anyone how much these visions were bothering him. Sure, he had told his friends, but they had no idea just how disturbing they were, and frankly, Pacey wasn't sure he wanted them to get the full, gory picture. There was so much going on with Monique, with this firestarter running around . . . Pacey didn't want to cause more problems just because he thought he might be going crazy.

But Andie was looking at him searchingly, and Pacey knew the girl would be able to tell if he was hiding anything from her. He took a deep breath. Maybe she'd be able to help him make some sense of the whole thing.

"Okay, well, I'm kind of embarrassed about this, but . . . it's the whole vision thing. They're really freaking me out."

Andie nodded seriously. "They're worse than you said they were, aren't they?" she asked.

"Yeah, actually, they are. I can't even describe it. It's like . . . the opening of *Saving Private Ryan*, almost. You know . . . slow motion, gory. I mean, these aren't just daydreams or passing thoughts. This is nothing that would ever even exist in my own head. That's what scares me, Andie. These don't come from any of my stored memories, or even my wildest imagination. These come from someplace entirely foreign. What if it's permanent?"

Andie shook her head. "That's not gonna happen, Pace. I mean, believe me, I know how the mind can be influenced by events and surroundings. What did Elolie say to you? That your mind was closed?" Pacey nodded. "Well, who knows. The power of suggestion is strong. Did you know that only ten percent of the human brain is active?"

"Are you serious?" Pacey asked. "Man, it's a wonder we're still on the planet."

"But what we do use, we use well," Andie said. "But that's why there's so much unexplained phenomena in the world. I mean, it may sound hokey, but not all psychics are full of it. That little kid in *The Sixth Sense*, he was just more open to everything around him because more of his brain was active. There's an actual gland that affects how much of your brain is used . . . I think it's the pituitary gland . . ."

"Okay, okay, McPhee, don't get all technical on me," Pacey said.

"All I'm saying is that it's not out of the question that more of your brain has become active," Andie said. "Thus allowing more things to filter in. It's not that these actual visions are permanent. But maybe you're just . . . more aware now. It's not such a bad thing."

"Well, when you put it that way . . ." Pacey said. Speaking of being more aware, the back of Pacey's neck suddenly felt prickly. He glanced over at the wings. In the shadows, just beyond the ballroom, stood Elolie. She wasn't wearing a mask, but she didn't need to; it was freaky enough just to look into her piercing eyes. She caught Pacey's gaze and smiled at him knowingly. He caught his breath and quickly looked away.

"Okay," he said to Andie nervously. "What say we spin on over to another side of the ballroom?" Before she could even respond, Pacey whirled Andie in the opposite direction. He didn't even know where he was going. Anything to move away from Elolie. She may not have meant ill toward him, but Pacey didn't want to risk any more awareness coming his way.

Meanwhile, Jack had found another dance partner: Joey. They were both keeping an eye peeled for the masked man, but neither wanted to admit to each other that it seemed like a lost cause. Monique was right; it was like looking for a needle in a haystack.

"Hey, where's Monique, anyway?" Jack asked. He had just seen Jen dance by with a stranger, but he hadn't seen Monique for quite a while.

Joey averted her eyes. Monique's secret was safe with her. She was sure that Monique and Tom were already in the tunnels. The four of them had agreed that Tom and Monique would go in first and find out where the final tunnel began, and then they would come back out to get Joey and Dawson. But Joey wondered if the plan was still the same, given that it was highly possible there was still a stranger skulking around in the voluminous house, out to get them.

"Um, I don't know," she finally said. "She's probably just a little freaked out. Maybe she's up in her room resting." Jack looked at her strangely for a moment. *What was Joey being so weird about?* Jack wondered.

However, before Jack could further probe at what was going on with Joey, a masked figure approached them. The two were startled for a moment, until they saw it was Dawson after he lifted the mask.

"At this rate, you guys are going to think that everyone's out to get you," Dawson said, chiding them for being nervous.

"I know," Joey groaned. "I don't even think I can remember what that guy's mask looked like at this point. Everything's blurring together. I mean, I can't even tell you guys apart with your masks on."

"Hey, Jack," Dawson said. "You mind if I talk to Joey for a second?"

"Oh, man," Jack replied. "What is it about me that makes guys think they can cut in on whoever I'm dancing with? It's the nice guy thing, isn't it? Cut off the nice guy." Jack was obviously kidding, so Dawson and Joey just laughed. "Don't worry about it," Jack said. "I'll just wander off into the crowd here and see if I can find myself an arsonist."

"Sounds good." Dawson smiled. He waited for a moment until Jack was farther away, and then he turned to Joey, taking her in his arms. They began to dance. Joey noticed how natural it was to dance with Dawson. They fit so well together, it was as if they were made for each other. But she pushed the thought out of her mind. This wasn't the time to be thinking about things like that, things that just confused her further.

"So," Dawson said. "Have you seen Monique anywhere? I wonder if she and Tom already went in."

"Maybe," Joey replied. "I haven't seen her for a while, not since we started looking for the guy. Any luck?"

"No. I hope Monique's okay. I wonder if something happened to her," Dawson said.

Joey shook her head. "Don't even think like that, Dawson." She knew that Dawson was always the hero under pressure, but at the same time, he could also blow things out of proportion when his imagination ran away with him.

Dawson could tell by the look on her face exactly what Joey was thinking. He could tell when her cynical gears started churning. "So," Dawson said nonchalantly. "I would think that even the critical Joey Potter would be pretty impressed with this whole scenario."

"The scenario of us being put in danger?" Joey asked. "Oh, yes, it's thrilling."

"No, there's nothing fun about us or our friends being in danger," Dawson said. "I guess I was just wondering if maybe this had sparked your belief in romance at all. Or even drama, for that matter. I mean, don't you appreciate the drama of what Monique is willing to do to save this place? It's like Scarlett O'Hara and Tara."

Joey took a deep breath. She knew exactly what Dawson was doing, and she wasn't going to be swayed by him just because he looked really good in a suit. He was poking at her for the thrill of the debate and she knew it. "I see what you're saying, Dawson," she began. "But this whole drama you speak of doesn't have anything to do with love—"

"Are you kidding me?" Dawson asked. "This is completely about John and Isabella."

"Yeah, those people are dead, Dawson. They might have fallen in love in this house, but that's all that remains. This whole thing, with the person sabotaging the plantation—that doesn't have to do with love, that has to do with money. With someone trying to screw Monique out of her home. Yeah, it's dramatic, but it's reality, not some fairy tale. It's typical modern behavior."

"What about Tom and Monique. They're in love," Dawson insisted.

"Sure they are, but Uncle Winston would never let them be together. I bet you anything if they actually came out as a couple, this town would spit on them. All these high society people are the same, Dawson."

"You don't know that, Joe. After all, Monique comes from money and she's not like that," Dawson said.

"Yeah, because her money's gone," Joey pointed out. "I know you think I'm trying to rain on your parade, but I'm not. I'm just saying there's a very good reason behind all of this stuff, in the long run, and it's not the lovesick soul of Isabella Percy coming back to avenge her lover."

Bayou Blues

Dawson shrugged as he spun Joey around. "Well, I know it's hopeless to argue with you. But you can't deny that the reason Monique is so attached to this plantation and its history has something to do with John and Isabella."

Joey cocked a smile at Dawson as he dipped her. No, she couldn't deny that. She just figured that one of the two of them had to be the realist. Otherwise, they might get in above their heads in this whole frightening mess.

"I can tell by your silence you're thinking about something," Dawson challenged her. Joey was about to open her mouth to fire a retort when a gloved hand touched her shoulder. She turned around to see a young man in full costume with a mask so detailed and expansive that she couldn't even see the color of his hair, or any other defining characteristics.

"Well, I'm stumped," Joey said. "Who is it?" The man didn't look like Pacey or Jack, despite the fact that Joey was having a hard time keeping everyone's masks straight.

The stranger leaned in close to Joey. For a moment, Joey was startled. All she needed that night was more strange behavior from masked men. But the man lifted his mask ever so slightly, just enough so that Joey could peek in and see his eyes.

"It's me, Tom," the young man said. "I'm trying not to get my cover blown."

Joey stifled a laugh. "Well, you picked the right kind of party. What's going on?"

"Is Monique in the tunnel?" Dawson asked.

"Yes," Tom whispered. "We finally pieced the torn part of the map together, so we found the last tunnel."

"That's awesome!" Dawson said. "So let's go." His eyes darted around the room. He wanted to make sure that the three of them got away to meet Monique in the tunnel before any of their friends saw them. He didn't enjoy keeping a secret from them, exactly, but Dawson wanted to make sure that he did his part to help Monique save her home.

Joey seemed to be reading his mind. She looked at Dawson and quietly asked, "Do you think we should find the others, maybe make something up about where we're going?"

Dawson shook his head. He knew this was all going to come out eventually, but now was not the time. Aside from that, the dance floor was far too crowded. With the costumes, Dawson wasn't even sure if they would readily find their friends, even if they tried.

"Let's wait," he said. "They're occupied looking for the masked man anyway."

"I hope they find him," Joey said. "I'd much rather they find him out here than we find him in the tunnels."

"No one knows about the tunnels except for the three of us and Monique," Tom assured them. "When Monique found that map, she didn't tell anyone. The only person who knew was her mother."

Joey nodded, understanding. Excited, she and Dawson took each other's hand and followed the masked Tom quickly off the dance floor.

Meanwhile, on the other side of the ballroom,

Jack, Jen, Pacey, and Andie had all finally caught up with each other. They were trickling out of the ball-room, completely paranoid at this point. Andie found herself hanging onto Jack, a gesture that had become somewhat of a habit. Jack looked down at her and smiled. After the whole warehouse incident, Jack and Andie had both been a little more under-standing of the other sibling's jittery side.

Jen grabbed Pacey's arm suddenly as she saw a man move in the shadows in the hallway beyond the ballroom. The figure was concealed by the darkness, but as he walked into patches of brightness reflected by the overhanging white lights, Jen could swear that his mask and build matched those of the firestarter.

"I think that's him," she hissed to Pacey. Pacey squinted, agreeing with Jen. He glanced at Jack for confirmation. Jack nodded in the affirmative. His heartbeat began to pick up. For a moment, the four friends didn't move. They couldn't, actually. It was like the moment in a dream when you are being chased by your killer but it feels as if your feet are caught in tar. Then Andie took a deep breath, and it seemed to trigger everyone. Like a singular unit, they burst forth from the ballroom, the girls lifting their long, rustling skirts, the boys pushing their masks off their faces so they could run undeterred. The friends moved lightly, hanging onto each other for balance as they practically skimmed over the floor, desperate not to be heard by the criminal they were chasing.

However, the masked man was running as well, and much faster than a group of four teenagers in formal wear could manage. He knew he was being chased, so the gang gave up trying to sneak up on him and broke into a full sprint. They had no idea where they were going; all they knew was that they were far enough away from the ballroom that no one would be able to hear them if they screamed.

Pacey was the first to barrel around the corner where the masked man disappeared. It was the back study of the mansion, presumably the study that Uncle Winston used. It was dimly lit by a small lamp on a side table by the couch, but Pacey got there just in time to see the man disappear . . . behind a wall? It seemed highly unlikely, but it happened before Pacey could even blink. It was as if a panel in the wall literally slid out of place, and then back in again as soon as the man stepped in.

"What? What?" Andie demanded, gripping Pacey's arm. She was breathless, and couldn't see anything. She peered into the dim room, confused. "What happened? Didn't he go in here?"

"He did," Pacey said. "And then . . . I swear, I know you're not gonna believe me, but it was like the wall was on a trigger. The guy went behind it, and . . . it's like a freakin' trigger, à la Scooby Doo."

"Really?!" Andie's voice held a mixture of excitement and horror. She ran up to the wall, groping along the paneling for the trigger.

"Do you think that will really work?" Jen asked. "I mean, did he actually disappear behind the wall?"

"I swear to God," Pacey said.

Jen looked at Pacey for a moment. He had such a determined look on his face, a fire she had rarely seen in him before. He had changed, the way people do when they go through something intense or frightening. She understood with certainty that Pacey was serious now about helping and getting to the bottom of things, and she also understood that he could. Maybe all of this was true . . . maybe Elolie really had opened up his mind and Pacey was experiencing things now that none of them could explain, let alone understand.

"If anyone could find the trigger, actually, I bet it would be Pacey," Jen said.

Jack and Andie took a moment to look at Pacey. Jen was right. However uncanny the reasoning might be, Pacey was definitely tuned into something in this house. Jack remembered again what the woman had said to him in the streets.

"You guys," he said tentatively. "I really don't want to freak anyone out, but I want to get this off my chest. This woman in the street . . . maybe she was crazy, maybe not, but she told me . . . she told me that someone was in danger, and that I had to warn them. I don't know if it's—"

But before he could finish, Jen cut him off, her eyes wide. "Okay. Scary. Consider us warned, and let's not even think of the consequences. Let's just make sure we keep each other safe. I'm not taking chances."

"Okay," Andie said, all business. "Pace, you try to find the trigger. We're gonna go back through the ballroom and see if we can catch the guy on the other side."

Pacey nodded, not believing that he had actually

become the guy who was supposed to find the secret trigger in the hidden door. How had this happened to him? His three friends ran out, leaving Pacey alone in the dim, silent study.

Pacey rubbed his hands together. "Okay," he said to himself. "Let's go." He put his hands on the panel, feeling every inch of it, silently praying he would find the trigger in time. He had a feeling that, wherever the man had disappeared to, it was a place where he'd put someone in danger. Someone dear to Pacey.

18

The Final Expedition

The wind whistled through the tunnel like a mad banshee. Joey shivered as the cold whipped around her, blowing the skirt of her strapless gown up like an open umbrella. She quickly pushed it down, knowing she really should have changed before entering the catacombs under the mansion. Evening wear wasn't exactly meant for traipsing around tunnels. Neither were the high heels that suddenly pinched her toes. They definitely weren't meant to walk over uneven ground.

Dawson could feel Joey shivering beside him, so he slipped off his tuxedo jacket, putting it around her shoulders. If this were the prom, she'd probably have worn it that way, but instead, she put her arms into its sleeves and wrapped it around herself tightly, protectively. She didn't want to admit it to Dawson, but she was scared.

Tom was in front of them, leading the way. Watching his shadow bob ahead of them in the strange lantern light, Joey could feel her heart beginning to beat faster. If anything had the makings of a bad horror movie, this was it: Teenage kids wandering around old Civil War tunnels looking for buried treasure, while someone lurked in the dark stalking them. She was wearing the classic get-killed-in-your-high-heels attire. The only thing missing was a chain-saw.

The wind shrieked again! Joey jumped.

"You okay?" Dawson asked, concerned. He knew that Joey was probably spooked by everything that had happened in the last hour, but somehow seeing a man flee the scene of the crime made everything palpable for him. It meant that there was actually *someone* behind the fire, behind everything that had happened at the Percy Plantation, instead of random evil unleashed because some bones had been disturbed. It meant that the only real evil here was in some man's heart. The question was: Whose?

"Dawson, what if whoever started the fire is down here with us?" Joey asked in a voice so small that it almost didn't sound like her.

"Joe—"

Tom interrupted. "No one knows about these catacombs but us. That much I'd swear on. The Confederates knew what they were doing when they decided to hide the gold down here. If we didn't have a map, you guys know there's no way we could have come down this far." He turned his attention back to the path in front of them, straining his eyes. "I left Monique up at the bend ahead. That's where we'll divide up." He picked up the pace then, in a hurry to get back to the woman he loved.

"How are your feet doin'?" Dawson was aware that Joey was beginning to limp.

"I'm okay."

But she was still shivering. Dawson put his arm around her, rubbing her arms, trying to warm her up.

"Still cold?"

"A little." Joey smiled up at him. Having his arms around her made her feel safe. Dawson always had a way of making everything okay. She put her head on his shoulder, thankful.

Up ahead it was totally dark, and Tom started to get worried. "I told her to wait here. I left her with a flashlight—"

"—That went out. You were supposed to check the batteries." Monique walked out from the shadows startling Tom, which made her laugh. "And you told *me* not to get scared."

"I'm not scared," he protested. "At least not for me."

She could see the worry in his eyes, which made her soften. She kissed him sweetly.

Dawson and Joey found themselves looking at the ground, not wanting to intrude. Love was funny that way, sweet and magical, but somehow private, Joey thought. And though she might not be in love at the moment, seeing love, or talking about it, always gave her hope that it would happen to her again—though she'd never admit this to Dawson. Dawson grabbed her hand then, squeezing it tight. Could he read her mind, she wondered. She looked up at him with her trademark half-cocked grin.

"What?"

"What am I thinking?"

Dawson knew she was serious, and he also knew he could tell her. He smiled at her devilishly.

"You actually know, don't you?"

"I know you."

The words were so simple. Joey wondered why the truth was always like that.

"Tom, light the other lantern and give it to them." Monique said, pulling out Sheridan's map. She drew Joey and Dawson closer. "We're here, obviously right before this gaping hole in the map that so inconveniently makes this harder. Unfortunately, it looks like the treasure is here, beyond these tunnels."

Joey's eyes followed Monique's finger trace over the tunnels, over the gaping hole in the map that was a mystery, then to the treasure that was just beyond it, in a small room off to one side of another tunnel.

It looked so close, Dawson thought.

Tom handed Dawson the lantern, adding, "It's not as close as it looks, man. We've found out by a lot of trial and error that this map is definitely not to scale. We also don't recommend separating; it's all twisty and windy down here. I don't want to have to send out a search party for either of you."

"What do we do if we find the treasure?" Dawson asked.

Bayou Blues

Monique grinned, "What do you think?"

Dawson smiled back, knowing that this one act would change Monique's life, save her home, make everything right in the Percy world again.

"So why are we just standing here?" Joey wanted to know.

"We're not," Dawson said, pulling Joey into the tunnel on the right, lantern blazing, determined to find John Sheridan's treasure.

They hadn't gotten very far when a strong wind came whipping through the tunnel again. Joey grabbed her dress, while Dawson tried to shield the lantern. Neither act really worked, Joey's skirt blowing up and the lantern blowing out about the same time. They stood in the darkness for a moment before saying anything.

"Got the Marilyn thing under control?" Dawson said, trying not to laugh.

"You do know that strapless gowns were invented by men to torture women."

"Lookin' at you Joe, I swear it was to torture men."

Joey could feel Dawson smiling in the dark.

"Unless you have a match, you better catch up with Monique and Tom. They can't be that far down the other tunnel yet," she said, changing the subject.

"You sure?"

"Go before they get too far away. " Joey let go of his hand then, and could feel him hesitate for a moment before heading off quickly the way they came.

Without his hand in hers, the wind felt a little colder and the tunnel suddenly seemed darker. She

213

knew this was all in her mind; he'd be back in a few minutes and they'd wind down this tunnel until they either came to its end, or found the treasure. Maybe if she just sat down for a minute her shoes would stop pinching and she'd stop scaring herself.

She put her hands out in front of her, trying to find the wall. Before the lantern had gone out, she thought she'd seen a rock that she could sit on. She groped in the dark, making sure not to trip and fall. After ten steps, she realized she must be going deeper into the tunnel. She strained her eyes to see something, anything, but it was still pitch black. No amount of straining would produce any kind of visibility. She turned to the right on instinct, knowing the wall had to be close-by. She inched toward it.

A warm breath fell over her and she stopped, suddenly terrified.

"Dawson?" she whispered, hoping.

And then someone grabbed her. He was rough and strong. She managed to get out a scream before he clenched his hand over her mouth, dragging her kicking, gasping for air. She wouldn't go without a fight. She tried to anchor her feet to the ground, but her heels only managed to put her more off-balance. This man was really strong, and if he held onto her this way much longer she would black out.

In the next tunnel, Dawson had just caught up with Monique and Tom when they heard Joey scream.

"Joey?!" Dawson shouted, panicked.

Before he could even think, he was running, trying to find his way back to her. He ran blindly in the dark, managing to avoid bumping into walls by touch and some sixth sense he didn't even know he possessed. He'd never been so scared, nor felt so helpless.

"Joey?!" he shouted.

Why didn't she answer?

Behind him he could hear Tom and Monique trying to catch up, and though logic told him he should wait for them, it would be easier to find her with light, he couldn't be logical now. The girl he loved in one form or another his entire life was in real danger and it was his fault. He'd left her alone.

"Joey?!" he shouted.

His voice echoed back at him, mocking him.

He ran faster, wondering why he wasn't there already. As he maneuvered around another corner, there was the faintest bit of moonlight coming from what looked like the end of the tunnel. As he adjusted his eyes, he could see Joey being dragged out by some masked man, the same masked man who set fire to Isabella Percy's study.

"Joey!"

Joey couldn't see Dawson, the masked man's grip was too tight. She was gasping for air, trying to keep her balance so he wasn't choking her. If only she could scream, bite him, anything, but she could barely breathe, fighting back tears from sheer terror.

The masked man pulled her out into moonlight, going through some sort of door. The ground was wet below her, and she struggled harder to keep upright, as the man forced the door closed.

All light disappeared from the tunnel when it shut.

Dawson slammed his body against the door. He wasn't thinking anymore. He just knew he had to get to her before anything else happened. He slammed his body against it again. It wouldn't budge. He pushed, clawed, bloodying his own fingers in futility.

"Dawson! Stop!" Monique pulled at his hands.

He looked at her, searched her face for any sign of hope.

"We'll find a way out," she told him.

Tom, who had both lanterns, now lit the second one, and illuminated the whole area. The door was solid wood, old, and at least three inches thick, but at the top of the door there was loose dirt. They quickly began digging until they had a hole big enough for someone to fit through.

Tom gave Dawson a boost. Dawson grabbed the top of the door for support, and pushed through the moist dirt, forcing his way out. He tumbled to the ground below with a thud. Looking around he realized he was in the middle of the bayou. Miles of swampland all around. It was overwhelming. His eyes searched everywhere. Where was she?

"Dawson, are you okay?" Monique yelled out to him.

"Call the cops. Bring them out to the bayou. Now!"

The panic in his voice made Monique shudder. "We're on our way," was all she could manage to say.

"You sure you can run?" Tom asked her.

"Just don't let go of my hand."

He squeezed her hand tightly, and they began back the way they came. Time was of the essence.

19

Pandora's Box

Pacey banged his head against the wall in sheer frustration. The trigger had to be somewhere in this study. The more time it took to find the secret passageway, the greater the odds would be that they'd never catch the man who set the fire. Even if Jen, Andie, and Jack got to the other side in time, the ballroom was filled with masked men, so their firestarter could easily disappear again.

It shouldn't be that hard, Pacey thought. He could swear that all the man did was touch the marble bust on the mantel and the wall had opened.

Pacey moved the bust every which way without breaking it, even going as far as to pull on the bust's ears and poke at its eyes, like some bad Three Stooges movie. He hated being so close, and yet so far away from solving this mystery. The only thing that consoled him was the fact that they'd all seen a regular, ordinary man flee the fire, so he was fairly sure that voodoo really had nothing to do with any of the events that had happened since they arrived.

"Just open, damn it!"

Pacey started pounding on the wall. He went from one side of the room to the other, methodically. As he got closer to the mantel, he realized it was futile, and just stared at the offending wall.

"You aren't going to open, are you? You know you're protecting the wrong guy, right?" Pacey couldn't believe he was trying to appeal to the wall's sense of morality.

And it worked. The wall swung open.

"Who knew you had a conscience?"

"Who are you talking to?"

The voice startled him. It was Monique, who came tumbling out of the wall, Tom right behind her.

"What were you guys doing in there?" Pacey realized things were getting stranger and stranger.

"We'll explain later. Right now I need to call the police. Joey's in trouble."

Monique picked up the phone and dialed.

Tom followed her, but Pacey grabbed him, stopping him. "Tom, what is she talking about?"

"The guy who set the fire has Joey. Dawson's trying to catch him, but he needs help."

"Where are they?!"

"Somewhere in the bayou. One of Sheridan's tunnels came out there." Tom showed him the map, pointing to where they'd last seen Dawson. Pacey grabbed it from him, staring at the map, trying to make sense of the situation.

"No, I can't hold. It's an emergency. Someone's life is in danger," Monique said into the phone. "Damn it. This is nine-one-one for God's sake, don't put me on hold!" But it was obvious they had. "Tom, try dialing on one of the other lines."

Tom headed out into the foyer for a phone.

Pacey knew he couldn't stand there and wait. He had to do something to help. He grabbed their lantern and started for the tunnel.

"Pacey, wait!" Monique yelled after him as the wall began to close between them.

"Just get them help," he said. And he was gone.

Now standing in the tunnel, Pacey tried to get his bearings. The map indicated he should head to the right. He walked quickly, then started to run. Someone had Joey, and he was nowhere near Dawson to help him get her back. He ran faster, winding deep into the bowels of the house.

Tom found Monique sitting by herself in the study. Her knees were drawn to her chest, and she looked like she was trying to stay warm, but Tom knew it was more than that.

"They told me you got through."

"Yeah," she said in a small voice.

"What's wrong? Where's Pacey?" he asked her.

"He took off below to help Dawson. I couldn't stop him."

"It's going to be okay, Mo." He took her into his arms.

"What if something happens to her, Tom?"

"The police will be here soon."

"But what if they don't get here in time?" Monique looked up at him, tears brimming.

Tom didn't answer her.

In the catacombs, Pacey was thinking the same thing, wondering if he'd ever get to the end of this tunnel that led aboveground. It seemed endless. He stumbled then, barely able to keep himself upright, his lantern rolling across the ground. He quickly chased after it as it gained momentum, rolling faster and faster down the incline, heading left and right as if knowing where it was going. It seemed to have a mind of its own, and when he finally caught up with it, he realized he had no idea where he was. Cold wind whipped at his face. The wind certainly had to come from above, he reasoned, so he didn't turn around, descending even deeper into the catacombs.

Aboveground, Joey struggled for her life. She was beginning to lose consciousness and flailed at the masked man, but his grip was still too strong. He clenched his hand even tighter over her mouth and nose, depriving her of needed oxygen. He was killing her, she thought, and there was nothing she could do about it. Telepathically, she tried to speak to Dawson, tell him where she was, willing him to her, hoping he really could read her mind. *By the tree house,* she thought, before blacking out.

Dawson stopped running. For the first time in five minutes he had no idea where to go. Up until that point he'd been running on blind instinct. Panic gripped his heart. Something had happened. The thought that this man could have . . . He wouldn't let himself think that. If he did, he'd lose it and he'd be no good to her. The last noise he'd heard had been this way, he thought. He looked down at the marshy ground for any kind of clue, and that's when he saw it—the tree house, which was in a large oak tree. The roots of the tree stuck out all over the place like a snake's nest. Something drew him closer and he started to crawl over the roots. Something caught his eye. A piece of Joey's black dress snagged in tangled roots. She had just been here!

He searched the base of the tree fervently, discovering a solitary set of footprints. The prints sank deep into the ground. The masked man was obviously carrying her, which meant she had to be unconscious. *Only unconscious,* he prayed. He quickly followed the footprints.

Pacey stared at Sheridan's map, then at his surroundings. He was still lost. Not that he ever really knew where he was since he began this ludicrous journey down Alice's rabbit hole. He closed his eyes in pure frustration, then opened them, asking the heavens for a sign. He couldn't just be trapped down here while Joey's life was in danger. That's when he reached the end of the tunnel.

A dead-end.

No door.

No hole that led to the outside world.

He'd taken the wrong tunnel, and would have to head back who knows how far? He clenched his jaw, anger overtaking him. He kicked at the wall that just ended. That kept him from the outside world. He kicked harder and harder, just burning off steam. And to his surprise his foot broke through, getting caught in the wall.

"Great."

He pulled at it, but it wouldn't come out. So he sat down and braced his other foot against the wall and pulled with all his might. When his foot finally broke free, he rolled back from the wall, which suddenly gave way to a small avalanche. Pacey quickly put his hands over his head, shielding himself. When the dirt finally stopped falling, he was surprised to see some sort of room in front of him.

He wiped the dirt away from his face, blinking to see if the vision was really real. A Confederate flag was draped across the wall of the room, an ammunition supply below it, a book beside it. In the middle of the room were bedrolls; someone had actually slept here. John Sheridan, Pacey thought as he made his way into the room, careful not to disturb anything. This room, cave, was a place out of time. Pacey thought of the story Jen had told them. Maybe this was where Sheridan had guarded the Confederate gold. It could be right here. He grabbed his lantern to get a better look.

As he got to the center of the room, something near one of the bedrolls caught his eye. It was a tin box, the tin box from his vision. Pacey felt a lump in his throat. He'd just been able to convince himself that it was all mumbo jumbo. If this box started to float and blood started to ooze out of it—What then? Pandora's box, he thought. Open it and unleash evil on the world.

Strange thing was that he couldn't stop himself. He found himself picking up the box, dusting it off. He turned it over. The initials J.S. were engraved on the bottom of the box.

"John Sheridan. Your box. Your room. Your evil? I don't think so." Pacey tried to pry open the box. Rust and age kept it closed. "Okay, this feels a little familiar, but no oozing blood, so that's a good sign. Just need something to . . ." He found an old spoon on the floor. "That'll do it." He ran the handle of the spoon through the crack that went around the box, then tried again. This time it opened easily.

Inside the box was a letter addressed to Isabella Percy. Pacey sat down on the bedroll and opened it. The paper was old and yellowed. He unfolded it very carefully and began to read:

My dearest Isabella,

If you are reading this, I am surely dead. When the Union soldiers captured the plantation yesterday, I was unable to protect you. They tortured you to get to me, and I couldn't stand by and watch you suffer. Though I know you think me wrong, I am taking them to the gold. I am doing this in exchange for your life. Major Douglas has promised me your safe-keeping for my cooperation. I think he is a man of his word.

You know as well as I do, that as soon as I give them the gold they will no longer need me,

*and I will be executed. I do not mind this,
knowing that you are safe. My only regret is
not marrying you when I had the chance. I
love you more than life, and would give up a
thousand treasures for you.*

*Please, my darling, do not cry for me. I know
that we will be together someday. And on that
day the stars will shine brighter, and God will
marry us. That's all that matters. You are my
heart, my love, my everything.*

John

Pacey looked around at his surroundings, knowing this was probably the last thing Sheridan saw.
War was cruel, he thought. Then he thought about
his vision. There was obviously a reason he was
here. He took the letter and the box with him, heading back the way he came.

20

Deliver Me Unto Salvation

Joey opened her eyes and all she could see
was stars. Hundreds of them shining brighter than
she'd ever remembered. They seemed to beckon to
her. She wondered if she was in heaven for a
moment, then began to feel her body. It felt bruised
and wet, and she realized she was still alive. She
groaned in pain. A hand quickly went over her
mouth.

"If you scream, you're dead," the masked man
whispered.

She felt herself nodding, wondering what kind of
surreal world she'd fallen into. Why had he taken
her, and was he going to kill her? What did he want?

"He'll find me," Joey whispered.

"Shut up!" He raised his hand to strike her.

"No!"

Dawson came out of nowhere, tackling the man. They tumbled and rolled, until they fell into the water. But the masked man was bigger and stronger than Dawson, taking him down in one punch.

Though he was in pain, Dawson wouldn't stay down. He was fighting with strength he never knew he had. He leaped out at the man again, a rage filling him that Joey had never seen. He swung and struck at the man, who managed to duck and get in another punch. Dawson went down again. This time a little harder.

"Dawson!"

It took him a second to get his wind back. "Run, Joe! Now!" He struggled to his feet.

The masked man went for Joey again. Dawson managed to pull him off her, and they tumbled again into the water. Joey tried to run, but her heels just slipped underneath her. She went down again, this time struggling quickly to get her shoes off her feet. She wasn't going to be a fatality in a horror movie. That's when she heard a splash and looked around. She couldn't see anything.

Dawson heard the same splash, but was closer to it. He could see that it was an alligator coming their way. He struggled to get up, but the masked man tackled him this time, pushing his head underwater. He was trying to drown him. Dawson struggled, flailed, managed to push him away. Toward the gator.

The man finally saw it, and started to flee, but it was too late. Snap! The gator had the man's pant leg, and pulled him off-balance. He fell into the water again, and didn't surface. The gator was actually holding him down, not letting go of his pant leg as it burrowed deeper into the swamp. The man struggled, kicking to free himself, finally jerking his leg so hard that his pants ripped, and he was able to surface. He gasped for air. That's when Dawson punched him hard, square in the jaw. He went down, out cold.

Dawson pulled him onto land, then searched the water for the gator, but it had disappeared. It hadn't come after them. That's when he began to wonder if that was the gator Pacey had told them about.

"Dawson!" Joey ran to him as fast as she could, throwing her arms around him.

He could feel her body trembling against his as he enveloped her in his arms. "It's okay."

He held her tight.

"It's not okay. He could have killed you."

Dawson knew she was right, but it didn't matter anymore. They were safe. "But he didn't."

She stared into his face then.

"What?"

"What took you so long?" And she smiled through tears.

Dogs began barking in the distance. They looked out toward the mansion and saw flashlights approaching. Finally, help had arrived. With no way to signal them, they both yelled out, "Over here!"

In the distance they could hear Tom's voice, "I hear them."

Dawson smiled down at Joey, then looked at the masked man, who was still out cold.

Joey followed his gaze. "Who do you think it is?"

"There's only one way to find out," Dawson said, bending down to take off his mask.

"Be careful."

He took it off, and stepped back in shock.

"Oh my God."

"Why? Why would he do it?" Dawson wanted to know.

That's when Tom arrived, police in tow. "You guys okay?"

"Yeah. Where's Monique?" Dawson asked.

"Back at the mansion, why?" And that's when Tom saw who was on the ground. He blinked, making sure he actually saw what he thought he saw. It was Winston Percy. "*Monique's uncle!* Son of a bitch!"

"You know this guy?" one of the policemen asked.

"Yeah."

Another policeman came forward with a walkie-talkie. "What do you want me to tell them?"

The first cop took the walkie-talkie from him, and spoke into it. "We've got the suspect in custody. The kids are okay. We're headed back your way. Over." The radio crackled.

"Roger." Monique, Pacey, Jen, Andie, and Jack were crowded around the policeman with the radio in front of the mansion. "Your friends will be back here shortly. Why don't you step over there and wait, let us do our jobs."

"Can't we do anything?" Pacey asked.

"I need a statement about the fire."

Jack volunteered, heading over to one side with the policeman, recounting the evening. Not that it made any sense.

Monique just looked out at the bayou. She needed to see with her own two eyes that her cousin's friends were safe.

"It's not your fault, you know." Jen put her arm around her cousin.

"I know."

Pacey took this moment to hand the tin box to Monique.

"What's this?"

"It belonged to John Sheridan. I found it in the tunnel I was in. There's a letter inside. I think you should read it, and then I think we should find Elolie."

"What about the treasure?" Monique asked.

Pacey shook his head no. "Confederate flag, ammo, bedrolls, but no gold."

Monique was devastated. After everything that had happened that night, to know that there was no treasure meant that there was no hope. She wouldn't be able to save her home. She opened the box and then Sheridan's letter. She read it slowly, and by the time she finished she was crying. She handed it back to Pacey.

"What did it say, Pacey?" Andie asked.

"Basically, he traded the gold and his life for her safety. She just never got to find that out."

"Wow. That's really sad. What does that have to do with Elolie?"

"You're the one who said we only use like ten percent of our brains. What if whatever Elolie did to me gave me a chance to right a wrong? To get this information to Isabella?" Pacey asked.

"I thought you didn't believe in ghosts."

"I don't know what I believe in anymore, but there's a reason I had those visions, right?"

Andie couldn't disagree with him. New Orleans, she'd discovered, was a strange place, where the dead stayed with the living, where magic was both good and bad, and nothing really made any sense. That's when she saw who the police had in custody. They all saw who was cuffed and being shoved into the back of a police car.

Monique was in shock. Tom came toward her, wanting to shelter her, but she just ran, into the house, slamming the door behind her, trying to get around the guests from the ball, as she ascended the stairs to her room.

"Monique!" Tom yelled after her, running to catch her.

Jen, Andie, Jack, and Pacey could only watch. Pure disbelief kept them where they were. That's when they saw Dawson and Joey, both draped in police blankets, muddy and bruised, but okay. They all ran toward them. Jen hugged Dawson first, while Jack hugged Joey. Then Andie hugged them both, and soon they were just one big mass.

"Hey Potter, can you breathe in there?" Pacey joked. He was on the outside, just thankful that his friends were safe.

"Come here, you." Joey hugged him tight. Then Dawson did the same.

"One hell of a night, huh?" Dawson said, still in shock.

"Do you guys know what happened?" Jen asked.

Dawson looked at the police car, at Winston Percy, a man they had all trusted. "Kind Uncle Winston apparently isn't so kind. He made a deal with Stetcher's dad to buy the place for a pretty penny, using Stetcher Junior as a pawn to get what he wanted. He told Junior that if he loved Monique he'd convince her to sell, confiding in him that the place was going to be foreclosed on. But Monique wouldn't sell. Stetcher Senior found out and figured he didn't care who he bought the plantation from and could wait for foreclosure. That's when Winston Percy panicked. He knew he had to act fast or he'd lose everything."

"So he planted the soldier's bones and started this mumbo jumbo about voodoo and Isabella Percy's curse to scare her into selling?" Jack said, knowing where this story was going.

"Yeah."

"The only problem was he didn't count on us. He thought we'd come down and distract Monique. Help his cause, but instead we started snooping around. So he tried to scare us, figuring if he got through to us, we'd get through to her," Joey said.

"But he didn't know about Sheridan's map, so you ran into him belowground, and he panicked," Pacey concluded.

"Something like that." Joey smiled, happy to be alive.

"Speaking of Sheridan's map, what do you guys say we find that treasure?" Dawson pointed back to house.

Pacey realized that Dawson and Joey hadn't been there for the big reveal. "There is no treasure, man. Well, there was, but this guy sort of sacrificed it for the woman he loved." He handed them Sheridan's letter.

They read it, both touched by John Sheridan's words.

"Amazing what you'll do for love," Dawson said.

"Yeah, it is," Joey said, taking Dawson's hand. "Let's go inside and talk to Monique. This must be really hard for her." Joey suddenly thought about her own father, who had betrayed her. Maybe if she told her about him it wouldn't hurt so much.

They all headed into the mansion, nonplussed by the ball that seemed to be in full swing. How did all these people miss all the drama that had just happened outside? It seemed so unfair, Jen thought. Her cousin was about to lose everything—couldn't these people just go home? They ascended the grand staircase.

In her room, Monique was still crying. She just couldn't pull it together. Tom had told her everything, and it broke her heart. She had loved her uncle, and to know that money meant more to him than her life . . . Nothing made sense anymore.

"Please stop. Take it back. Tell me you're lying, Tom." But she knew he wasn't. He would never lie to her. He genuinely loved her and like John Sheridan, he would give his life for her.

There was a small knock on the door, and then Jen

came in. "My friends are here, and we just wanted you know that if there's anything we can do—"

"I wish." More tears spilled from Monique's eyes.

Joey walked over to Monique. "Can I talk to you?"

"She needs to get some sleep. Can we talk about this tomorrow?" Tom said.

"It's okay, Tom," Monique reassured him.

Joey sat on the bed next to her. Everyone else stood in the doorway. Tom looked at Joey, skeptically. Nothing she could say could take the sting away from the night.

Then Joey opened her mouth. "I wouldn't presume to tell you how to feel, no one can do that. And though we come from very different worlds, we do have something in common. Someone I loved betrayed me, like your uncle did you. For me it was worse, it was my father. If anyone would have told me that my father would put the rest of my family in danger, as well as my friends, I would have told them they were crazy. But he did, all in the name of money. Our family business burned down because of him. He was like this narcotics smuggler. He's serving three to ten in our local penitentiary."

Monique stared at her, not knowing what to make of her story.

"I'm telling you this because my world didn't end. Mostly because of them." She indicated her friends across the room. "The family you were born with can let you down, but the family you choose usually doesn't. I try to remember that every day." Joey put Tom's hand in Monique's. "I just thought you should know that."

233

"Thanks." Monique appreciated everything Joey was saying, not that it hurt any less. Maybe a little less.

"We'll be outside if you need us," Joey squeezed Monique's other hand before heading out the door. The rest of the gang followed. Jen was the last one out, closing the door behind her. The last thing she saw was Tom wrap his arms around her cousin, offering her the comfort of his love.

In the hallway, everyone stared at Joey.

"That was really great, Joey," Jen said. "Thanks."

"Hey, I'm not going to see her again, so what do I have to be embarrassed about?" She was being sardonic and they all knew it. "Okay, you'd do the same for me, right?"

Jen had to laugh. "What, and tell everyone about my sexual exploits? . . . No."

Now everyone laughed.

"So what now?" Andie asked. "It'd be weird to go back to the ball."

Pacey still wanted to find Elolie. The letter was burning a hole in his tuxedo pocket. Though everyone here had read it tonight, there was someone still waiting for it. "Andie, you know that thing I talked to you about outside? Well, you want to come with me?"

"That sounds ominous," Jack said.

"You're welcome to come, man."

Jack had had enough adventure for one night. He was going to read a book in the study. Jen was up for that, then she could still be close to Monique.

Dawson and Joey looked at one another.

Somehow a shower seemed more appropriate, Joey thought.

"I'm with you, Joe. Let's go."

"I didn't say anything."

Dawson tried to suppress a huge grin. "Like I said, I know you."

They started down the stairs. "You are not the great Karnak."

"I can read your mind. Really."

"Okay, what am I thinking now?"

"Joe, you're making me blush."

"Shut up."

Pacey and Andie watched them go. Hearing their banter made everything seem sort of normal again, Andie thought. Except for the fact that she and Pacey were going to try to talk to the dead right now. They headed toward the back stairs that led to the kitchen.

"You sure you want to do this?" Andie asked.

Pacey had never been surer of anything in his life. He couldn't explain it, but he had to do this.

"You no have ta go down da stairs. We ready up hea."

The voice startled them. It was Elolie. She stood in the South Wing door, holding a small lantern. It was totally black behind her. Though Andie had thought the South Wing romantic only days ago, it now seemed really creepy.

"Pacey, maybe this is a bad idea."

"You don't have to come."

"I'm not going to let you go in there by yourself. Are you crazy?"

So she followed him, grabbing his arm. Again he thought, *This night just keeps getting stranger and stranger.*

"Ya visions led you hea, didn't they, boy?"

Pacey nodded. Elolie closed the door behind them.

"She knows ya foun' sometin'. She wants ta talk ta ya."

"Who are you talking about?" Andie asked.

Elolie laughed. Andie didn't think it was very funny. She also didn't think it was very funny that they were at the door to Isabella Percy's room. Whether she believed in ghosts or not, she didn't like being here in the middle of the night. Andie looked at her watch. It was close to midnight. The witching hour, as Jack called it.

"You're cutting off the circulation to my arm. Could you . . ." Pacey pulled at Andie's fingers.

"Sorry."

"I told you I could do this by myself."

"I'm not leaving you," Andie said, digging her nails into Pacey's arm.

"Ow. That's not funny." Though that actually did hurt, he had to admit he was glad Andie was with him. Elolie still scared him, and somewhere in the distance he could hear a clock strike twelve, which made this whole thing even spookier.

That's when the door to Isabella Percy's room opened by itself.

"She wan' ya ta go in," Elolie said, pushing at her young charges.

Pacey didn't like being pushed. Andie liked it even less. But they didn't have a choice.

The room was illuminated with a hundred candles, giving it a bright glow that was strangely soothing. There was also a small card table now in the center of the room, with three chairs around it.

"What's that for?" Pacey asked.

"Sit, fine out." Elolie took a seat and patted the one next to her.

Andie looked at the three seats, wondering how Isabella Percy knew she was coming. Pacey had some sort of calling, and Elolie, well, she was Elolie, but why would there be a seat for her, she wondered.

"Don' be scared. Other side knows much."

If that was supposed to soothe her, it didn't. Pacey yanked Andie into the chair.

"What now?" Pacey thought if the other side knew much, they must know about the letter, and probably read it already.

"Y' bein' simple. She waitin' a long time for dis. You know." Elolie stared at Pacey, looking inside him. He did know.

He pulled out the letter, and read. He read with passion, with the longing of a man who missed the only woman he'd ever loved. Like a man who knew he'd see his love again.

Wind began to blow through the room. It was warm and sweet, and blew the windows open. The candles danced to its song. Something was happening. Pacey and Andie looked around the room.

"She be with him," Elolie said.

Then all the candles went out, but the room still glowed brightly. The light floated out the window, into the sky. God had married them, Pacey thought. He took Andie's hand in his, thankful to share this with her. They had just witnessed a miracle.

They both walked to the window and stared out at the stars. Elolie sat behind them, knowing that the boy believed.

21

Believers

The next morning was a quiet one at the Percy Plantation. Joey woke early, quietly creeping out of bed and wincing in pain. Her body was still sore and bruised from the night before. She rubbed her head, hardly even believing the events that had taken place the night before. She didn't want to wake the others, yet. She wanted a moment alone to really absorb the morning. They were leaving that day. Joey felt like they had been there for months. They'd gotten so immersed in Monique's life and the history of the plantation that it seemed insane to be abandoning them now.

But they had done everything they could, Joey told herself as she stepped out on the stoop of the carriage house. They had even chased the criminal through the swamp with a live alligator, for crying out loud. Still, as Joey squinted into the morning sun, she couldn't help but feel that she had failed.

Suddenly, she felt a hand on her shoulder. She turned around to look at Dawson.

"Hey." She smiled.

"Hey," he said softly. The two of them didn't really need to say any more than that. The emotions of the evening before, and the danger the situation had put them in, had had such an impact on Dawson and Joey that there was really nothing they could say to each other that words would sufficiently express. Dawson rubbed her shoulder for a moment. He couldn't even manage to express to Joey how afraid he had been last night, and how very glad he was that they were standing on that step together, a new day ahead of them. They may have lost the big battle of saving Monique's home, but Dawson was comforted by the fact that at least they had helped in uncovering the deception that would only have further poisoned Monique's life.

Joey looked up at Dawson. "You think Monique's up yet?"

Dawson nodded. "I can't imagine that she slept at all. I think she's inside with Tom and Elolie."

"I'm going to go in and talk with her some more," Joey said. She held onto Dawson's hand for a moment before she walked toward the mansion.

Dawson gazed at Joey walking away. He was glad that Joey and Monique had made a connection the night before. Despite the fact that he had known Joey her whole life, and had been with her through all of the chaos, he knew that even he could never really understand what she had been going through. He was safely nestled in the middle class. Sure, his parents had gone through their rough patches, but they were happier now than ever. He had always wished he could look Joey in the eye and tell her that he completely understood her problems, but he didn't. He was glad that Monique would.

Joey found Monique sitting alone in the kitchen, quietly sipping a cup of tea. Joey paused for a moment in the doorway, wondering if she should go in. She knew how it was when you discovered everything you thought was true crumbled before your eyes; sometimes you just needed to be alone.

"Morning," she said softly. Monique looked up at her and smiled. Joey took this as a signal to enter the kitchen. She sat down across from Monique.

"Long night, huh?" Joey asked. Monique nodded. "Did Tom go home?"

"He just left," Monique said. "We were just talking in circles, trying to figure out what to do. And Joey, there's nothing. I mean, even if we pooled together all of our money, our savings, and my trust fund . . . even if we sold half the valuables in this house, I'm helpless to save this place. If only there weren't a time limit. The bank is breathing down our necks, and no one cares about family tragedies and betrayals at a time like this."

Joey remembered the day she and Bessie had gone to the loan officer together, the day she learned that Bessie had taken out a second mortgage on the house. She had been so horrified at the time, but

maybe that horror had propelled her to really work
with Bessie on getting the B&B off the ground. And
now the business was booming. She wished she
could offer Monique a similar solution, but that was
hardly something you could dream up overnight.
Not to mention the fact that Joey was sure Monique
wouldn't be able to pull together the funding to
restore the house. And, deep in her heart, Joey
couldn't help but feel that Isabella's Percy's wing
should remain untouched. That much respect should
be paid to her.

"I know how much you love this place," Joey
began. "My home back in Capeside . . . it's obviously
not as gorgeous as this, but it's where I grew up. It's
where all my memories of my mother are. It's the
place I'll always consider my home."

"And somehow you managed not to lose it,"
Monique sighed.

"But you know what?" Joey said. "The strength of
your character is going to get you somewhere in this
situation. I've seen few people in my life be as
devoted to something as you are to this house, to the
history behind it, even to Tom . . ." as Joey was talking, she realized that one of the only other people
she knew like that was Dawson. "That's truly romantic," Joey said. "And believe me, I don't think I
would have conceded that romance prevailed."

Was she losing the cynic in herself? Joey smiled,
wanting to find Dawson to tell him his assumptions
were correct and that she truly had gone through a
change, despite the fact that she knew how much
this would satisfy him.

"I guess I'll be glad knowing at least that I tried everything I could," Monique sighed. "But the fact remains that Michael friggin' Stetcher is going to insist on buying this place off. I can't believe how this whole thing panned out. The only person who's exactly who I thought he was is Tom, thank God. And you guys." Monique took Joey's hand. "I can't even tell you how grateful I am for everything you tried to do. I never would have thought that strangers could invest themselves so much in some-one's life."

Joey smiled back. "We're not strangers anymore. Come on, let's go see if we can find the others. We should spend some time together before we all leave." Joey also wanted to find Dawson. She needed to talk to him about the mental journey she'd been on. And while she didn't want to completely give in to him, she did want him to know that the events that had come to pass had definitely mattered to her, and certainly impacted her for the better. Having a little faith wasn't so bad, Joey decided.

Monique and Joey got up together and went into the foyer. Without the presence of Uncle Winston, the house now seemed even more desolate. They could faintly hear Elolie moving around upstairs, humming to herself.

"What is she doing?" Joey asked.

"She's blessing the house," Monique said. "So many evil things were happening here that Elolie wants to reverse the effects of it. Send it back to the evil tenfold, thus purifying the house."

Joey raised her eyebrows. "Well, that's cool," she

said. "I have a few people in mind I'd like to do the same thing to."

Monique laughed, but Joey could tell that her heart wasn't in it. She doubted that Monique would ever really be the same.

Monique and Joey heard something else besides Elolie stirring. Down the back hallway, they heard a spattering of footsteps that turned out to belong to Jack, Andie, Pacey and Jen. They all offered warm, sympathetic smiles to Monique. Jen went to hug her cousin.

"Morning, you." Jen said. "I don't think anyone slept that well last night."

Pacey shook his head. So many images had been running through his mind last night he couldn't sleep . . . but at least they had all been images he's actually seen, not disturbing ones planted in his memories.

"I'm sorry we couldn't help, Monique," Andie said.

"Yeah, me too," Jack added. "And about how things turned out with your uncle."

Monique shook her head. "Don't be sorry about that. It's good that the truth is out."

"Well, you can ask Jack," Jen said. "My house is always open. I'm sure Grams would love to have you. She took care of Jack for quite a while."

Jack nodded in the affirmative, smiling at Jen warmly.

Pacey wrinkled his brow. "Hey, where's Dawson for this warm and fuzzy moment?"

Joey shrugged. "I don't know. You know, I saw him at the carriage house earlier this morning, but I have no idea where he is now."

"I didn't see him back there," Pacey said. "And I've seemingly lost my psychic powers, otherwise I would lead you to him."

Just then, Dawson burst through the front door with Michael Stetcher. Monique stood up straight. She was obviously still upset that Michael had allowed himself to be a pawn to Uncle Winston, despite the fact that she herself had not seen through him.

"What are you doing here?" she asked.

Michael put up his hands, offering peace. "Listen, Monique, I don't know how many times I can tell you, I had no idea Winston was going over your head. I thought this was for the best. I see now I was wrong, and I've admitted that."

"You've known me my entire life, Michael." Monique shook her head. "I think you should have known better than anyone I would never have stood for that. And now I'm going to have to give this place up." She turned to walk away from them, obviously upset, but Dawson reached out and touched Monique's arm.

"Monique, just hear us out. I couldn't sleep last night, turning everything over in my mind. I ran into Michael outside—"

"I was just coming to check on you," Michael defended himself.

"Just let me stumble my way through this idea," Dawson said. "And tell me what you think when I'm done, okay?"

Monique nodded, suspicious, and sat down on the bottom step of the winding staircase.

"So we've realized at this point that there isn't any

hidden gold," Dawson began. "But I think we do have access to something that might be much more rewarding."

"No offense, Dawson," Joey said. "But I hope this isn't about the power of love or anything. Not that I haven't learned my own lesson in those powers, but I'm not sure that's what Monique needs to hear right now."

Dawson smiled mischievously at Joey. "No, Joe, that's not quite it, and I don't know whether to be flattered or perturbed that that's what you thought."

Joey grinned. She knew Dawson was messing with her.

"Anyway," Dawson continued. "As I was saying, I think that maybe there's something else you could draw from that would help you save the house."

"Really?" Monique said dubiously. "What's that?"

"The house," Dawson announced.

Andie piped in. "Dawson, we've gone this route. The three of us went to the Historical Society and we can't even get it declared a landmark."

Dawson nodded. "But that was before Pacey found what he did."

Pacey looked at Dawson and his eyes widened. He had known Dawson forever, and he knew exactly what his friend was thinking. Pacey started to break into a grin.

"The room." Pacey said.

Dawson nodded in reply, excited. "Exactly," he said. "The hidden room that Pacey found is full of stuff, stuff no one ever knew about. The weaponry in there, the uniforms—"

"There was a journal, too," Pacey interrupted. He had moved closer to Dawson, getting excited about this proposal. "It wasn't Sheridan's, but there was a journal kept by another soldier. I even saw sketches of battle plans."

"Are you serious?" Monique said slowly. She stood up from the stairs, coming to attention.

"Absolutely," Dawson said. "Now, if you take those individual items into account, it's not such a big deal, money wise. Still, they are fascinating pieces of another era. I really think that those pieces, combined with John and Isabella's story and the underground tunnels, would really draw people to this plantation."

"Yeah, does anyone know about those tunnels?" Jack asked. "Because they're amazing."

"Oh, my God. If I had just been visiting New Orleans and I didn't know you and you told me that I could take a tour through legitimate underground tunnels dug by the Confederate soldiers . . . I would definitely pay for that," Andie said.

Jack nodded. "Yeah, she totally would."

"Well, heck, I would, too." Pacey agreed. "I mean, now that my mind isn't dancing with images of bloody boxes, I would be crawling around down there, too. Those tunnels are awesome."

"Turn the house into a museum?" Monique asked.

"It's not as invasive as all that." Dawson shook his head. "I mean, you could obviously work it out that you didn't have to be on call all the time. You definitely need, and deserve, your privacy."

Monique nodded. "Well, that sounds great,

Dawson, but no matter what, I still don't have the money to invest to make much of anything out of this plantation. I can't handle it on my own, and Uncle Winston isn't coming back here—not under *my* roof."

Dawson glanced at Michael Stetcher, who nodded at him. "Well," Dawson said, "that's where Michael comes in."

"Monique," Michael began. "I've known you and your family for as long as I can remember. I feel awful about what Winston wanted to do to you, and believe it or not, I do appreciate your family's history. So I talked to Dawson about it, and I could manage to pay off your debt to the bank and give you back full ownership of the house, as long as you agree to pay me a percentage of the profits of the under-ground tours."

Monique couldn't help but be impressed. "Wow. You've really thought about this. Tours, huh?"

Michael nodded. "You hardly need to do anything down there to make it alluring to the public, Monique. The story itself will draw people in, and the tunnels already sound creepy and adventurous as it is."

Joey bit her lip. "Not to be the devil's advocate here," she said, "but doesn't it seem to go against everything to be exploiting John and Isabella this way?"

Dawson caught Joey's eye, smiling at her. He was surprised to see her defending the very love story she had once scoffed at. He supposed that near-death experiences could do that to a person.

You could see the wheels turning in Monique's mind. Finally, she spoke. "Actually, I don't even think it would be exploiting them. I mean, Elolie says their spirits watch over this place. They fell in love here, they died here . . . they don't want some other family moving in and taking that away from them, stomping through her old room, selling her old bed. I mean, it might sound cheesy, but I think that the more people who know about their love and their struggles, the more people who might appreciate the history of New Orleans."

"So do you think it's a good idea?" Dawson asked.

"I'm amazed that you guys put your heads together on this," Monique said. "I mean, I never would have thought of it. Well, I guess I never would have known, unless Pacey had found the hidden room."

"Pacey finding the room was the biggest deal," Dawson said. "That's what started the wheels turning."

"Well, why didn't you tell me?" Pacey asked with fake exasperation.

"Because," Dawson smiled. "After you finished tossing and turning and muttering in your sleep, you were out like a light, and snoring, I might add."

Joey groaned. "Oh, the snoring."

Pacey chuckled, admitting defeat.

"So . . . yes, I do think it's a good idea. I mean, I can't believe this is really possible, but everything you say makes sense. Obviously there are details to work out, but . . ." She turned to Michael. "You'd really do that? You'd really fund us?"

Michael nodded. "Monique, you have to understand, I was only looking out for you in this scenario. When I pressured you to sell, it was so you would be out of debt, not to make you leave. Winston led me astray, making me think it would be best for everyone. But now I see how you feel, and I just want you to be able to stay. I would do anything for you."

Monique smiled, blushing slightly. "I know that, Michael, and I'm sorry I—"

He shook his head, silencing her. "Don't worry about what I want or don't want, Monique. I need to deal with all that on my own. Despite how you may feel about me, I will always value my friendship with you. It's more important to me than what I can't have."

Monique nodded. Then her face broke into a grin. "Well, I can't believe this is happening!" she said. "I mean, I'm trying to go over every single thing that could go wrong in my head, but it all seems to fall into place."

"It will," Dawson said. "We can work out the math and the paperwork, but it will."

Jen hugged Monique. "Honey, that's so great!" she exclaimed. "Of course, you're still welcome in Capeside, but I know how badly you wanted to stay here."

Monique nodded. "I do, I really do. Tom's going to help me take care of the land, and Elolie's going to help take care of, well, me." She turned to Dawson and Michael. "I can't thank you enough. When I finally fell asleep last night, I never in my wildest dreams thought that something like this would be a possibility. Dawson, I am so extremely thankful that

you and your friends—all of whom helped me—
came into town with Jen. Who knows what would
have happened? I guess it's the one good thing
Uncle Winston did in this scenario."

Everyone laughed at that comment. Then
Monique grabbed onto Michael and hugged him
tightly. "And you, you are a generous soul. I'm sorry
I doubted you, Michael. I was in a bad position, and
I know you know that."

"Of course I do," Michael said.

"But I can't thank you enough. I really can't!"
Monique exclaimed, and she hugged him again.

Michael laughed, hugging her back. "All right, all
right, calm down. I'm still taking fifty percent of your
profits."

Everyone laughed at that. Jen watched Monique
and Michael. She could see by the look on Michael's
face that it was difficult for him to accept that Monique
would only think of him as a friend. She thought it was
very big-hearted of him to be so generous to Monique
when he obviously wanted more from her.

Monique turned around to face the rest of the
group. The look on her face was the happiest they
had seen Monique since they had arrived here.
Actually, it was the happiest Jen had seen her cousin
in years. The whole group was excited now; the kids
from Capeside really felt as if they had been a part of
something exciting, and Monique's dreams of saving
her home had been realized.

"Well, it's been such an awful week, I feel the need
to show y'all what kind of fun New Orleans can
really be," Monique said.

"Oh, Monique, don't worry about that. It's not as if we were exactly bored while we were here," Joey said.

"Believe me, we've had our fair share of adventure," Jack agreed.

"Oh, I'm not arguing about that," Monique laughed. "But we have got a few hours until you've got to take off, right? So let's go into town and have some real fun!"

"See, I knew this girl was related to me," Jen laughed, linking her arm with Monique's. "Let's get out of here."

Elolie stuck her head over the railing of the second-floor landing. It was as if she had appeared out of nowhere, as was her way. "Now listen to me, Miss Monique. Don' you be causin' no trouble in the city," she chided as Monique opened the front door.

Monique laughed, rolling her eyes as she and her new friends walked out the door. "Listen to her," Monique said. "She's put in charge of taking care of me and suddenly she's Queen Elizabeth."

"Well, if I remember you, she has reason to worry," Jen joked.

"That's right," Monique grinned. "You're leaving at dawn, right? Well, I'll have you back before then."

Dawson's eyes widened as he wondered if Monique was serious. Then he relaxed as he remembered two things: He was ready for anything now; and the beauty of having six people on a trip was that you could drive in shifts if someone got sleepy.

However, when the gang returned in the wee hours of the night to gather their bags together, even

Dawson wondered what on earth he had been thinking. Staying up all night before a long road trip! Still, the gang was jazzed to hit the road. Despite the fact that everything had turned out well, they were itching to get back to their own beds and their own dramas.

Jen hurled her duffel bag on the ground by Dawson's car. Dust billowed up around her, causing Jen to wave her hands in the air and cough.

"It's amazing," she said. "I could swear I didn't buy a single thing while I was here, but yet my bag seems to have grown, as if it had a life of its own." Dawson, who stood beside her, laughed gently. He turned around to face the house. It was barely dawn, and the stars still twinkled above the looming roof of the Percy mansion. Dawson gazed up at the stars, smiling to himself at the thought of John and Isabella being somewhere up there, relieved that their land was intact.

It was true; the Percy Plantation seemed to have entirely transformed since their arrival a few days earlier. Everyone could breathe a little easier now that Monique was going to be safe and content. Suddenly, the Percy Plantation didn't seem to be so weighed down with gloom. It was becoming once again what it had always been in its glory days; a fantastic, classical mansion with a beautiful history behind its heavy oak doors.

Dawson still wasn't sure if he believed in voodoo. Honoring the power of a true love story was one thing. Investing in the belief of voodoo was something else entirely. Still, he had seen things since he had been in New Orleans that he couldn't explain, especially with Pacey. He still wondered if Elolie had really cast a spell on Pacey that had opened his mind. Or had it merely been the power of suggestion? He could never be sure, he guessed.

Joey emerged from the house. She took in a deep breath of fresh air, smiling, and walked up to Dawson and Jen.

"Well, I never thought I'd be leaving this place feeling happy," Joey said. "Unless you count happy to leave."

"Yeah," Dawson nodded. "It turned out to be a very interesting time."

"See, " Jen said. "Aren't you glad I roped you guys into coming down here? If you hadn't come to visit my cousin with me, you never would have gotten trapped in hidden tunnels, almost killed in a gator-filled swamp, put out a fire, or caught a criminal."

"Never would have stayed up all night watching people swallow fire in the Quarter," Joey continued, laughing sleepily. "And even the dance part wasn't so bad. I mean, if I had stayed home, I just would have been sweeping up the hearth at the B&B."

Dawson had known from the beginning that Joey would enjoy the adventure, but he also knew that if he had predicted that, she would have knocked him out with a solid right hook. Okay, maybe not that violent, but still, she certainly wouldn't have appreciated him rubbing an "I told you so" in her face. He couldn't help it, though. It wasn't as if Dawson had set out to prove Joey wrong. It was that he knew her so well that he knew how Joey approached life; she was pessimistic, but then her big heart got the better of her. It was one of the things he loved about her.

Andie came around the corner from the guest-house, carrying a couple of bags. She loaded the bags into the trunk, arranging them neatly.

"Jack and I checked the carriage house twice just to make sure we didn't leave anything, so I think we're good."

Jen rolled her eyes. "Man, Andie, you are *so* anal. You know, if we left something, I'm sure that Elolie could have sent it back."

"Well," Andie smiled. "Jack, being paranoid and whatnot, wanted to make sure we weren't bringing anything back with us. You know. The evil."

"Speaking of," Jen said. "Where is Jack?"

"I think he's inside, actually. Looking for Elolie," Andie said.

"That Elolie," Jen shook her head. "Suddenly she's the guru for all the jaded boys."

"Yeah, I think Pacey was looking for her, too," Joey added. She hadn't really seen him since they'd returned from the city and piled into the guesthouse to take a group power nap.

"I don't know," Andie said. "Did anyone bother to make sure he was actually . . . awake? Because the pre-sunrise part of the day isn't exactly his finest hour."

Pacey was still inside, taking a final turn around the house. Despite the fact that the time he had spent there had been somewhat stressful for him, he couldn't deny that he felt a strong connection with the house now, and with the story behind it. In a way, he almost felt as if he had channeled some part of John Sheridan, as hard as that was for him to even admit to himself. Maybe he had truly become more open-minded, after all.

Jack came down the hallway behind Pacey.

"Hey, man," Jack said. "I think we're loading up the car."

"I figured. I was on my way out. Or are you looking for something else?" Pacey smiled.

Jack smiled back. "What do you, have the sixth sense now?" Jack didn't wait for Pacey's answer. "Yeah, I guess I was just waiting for some closure."

As if on cue, Elolie came around the corner. Pacey jumped a little, though he didn't know why; surely he should be used to Elolie appearing from out of the blue by now. Still, he didn't think he would ever get entirely used to a house like this one, particularly before the sun was up and the shadows were creeping across the walls.

"Does it take a lot of practice?" Pacey asked. "You know, scaring the heck out of people?"

Elolie smiled and came close to Pacey. "Not really," she said chipperly. "Easy wit' you, anyway. You scare."

Pacey nodded. "Yes, you know that's pretty much true. Well, I just wanted to thank you, you know, for the visit, and . . . for other things."

Pacey glanced at Jack, and Jack could tell that Pacey was still a little embarrassed to be talking about what had happened with him in front of everybody. After all, it was a little more out of the world than Pacey normally experienced. Jack cleared his throat.

"I just wanted to tell you, also," he said to Elolie, nervously, "that I had a lot of fear when I first came here. You know, about things I didn't understand. And I had wished for something—"

Elolie interrupted him with a wide smile. Her words rolled off of her tongue thick and low, a pleasant mumbling. "Good ting, huh, your wish came true."

Jack nodded, dazed. He still got the chills at Elolie's intuition. The woman leaned in close to Jack.

"She's a good friend of mine. Marie, she'd never do you harm," Elolie smiled.

Jack nodded. "Okay," he muttered to himself. "That is . . . closure." He nodded good-bye to Elolie and began to walk away.

"Good luck will follow you," Elolie said after them. Jack smiled and walked out the door to meet his friends.

Elolie turned to Pacey and began to walk toward the door with him. "It's good for you," she said.

Pacey stopped for a moment, examining the woman's face. He had forgotten that she had this way of picking up conversations where they'd left off, no matter how much time had passed. In fact, it was almost as if she existed in a completely different time frame altogether. He wanted to talk to Elolie more about what he'd been through, but Pacey was almost afraid to really press the issue with her; the questions he had for Elolie, well, he wasn't really sure he wanted to hear the answers.

Elolie must have known he was about to ask her

something. "You still doubt me?" she asked. Her voice went up into a high pitch, as if she couldn't believe Pacey would ever have any reason to be nervous around her.

Pacey smiled, and ducked his head. "I think it'd be pretty foolish of me to pretend that I hadn't experienced something. I feel foolish, to tell you the truth, for strutting into someplace I'm not even familiar with and claiming I know what's true and what's not. It makes sense to me now, what you said about the mind seeing what is always there. So . . . um . . . is it still . . . there?"

Elolie smiled and raised her hand gently to Pacey's forehead. She murmured something under her breath. Pacey wasn't sure what it was—it was in a language he couldn't understand, but he thought it might have been Creole. He stepped away on instinct, slightly afraid to go through another voodoo nightmare. But Elolie braced him, putting her hand on his shoulder.

"It's okay, boy. Your mind, it's open enough now," Elolie said, and she smiled at Pacey, the brightest smile he had seen on her the entire time he'd been there.

Monique came running down the stairs behind them. Jokingly, she said, "Elolie, now Pacey's a nice boy. No more tricks."

Pacey shook his head, chuckling. "No, no, it's okay," he said. "Whatever she did, I probably deserved it."

Monique grinned, linking her arm with Pacey as they walked out onto the front porch. "Well, I'm glad you've seen the good side of voodoo. By the way, you didn't say good-bye to Sebastian."

Pacey had to admit that the thought of the gator

still made him a little nervous. "Yeah," he said, shifting uncomfortably. "As much as I appreciate the bond that Sebastian and I shared, I gotta say that I'm going to keep our relationship on a need-to-see basis, and now is not really the time I need to see him. He's probably at his most hungry in the dead of night, right? But please, give him my regards."

Monique smiled at him. They were now outside, standing in front of Dawson's car with the others. "Well, thank you, Pacey, for everything you did. Thank you, *all* of you."

"Monique," Jen said. "You have thanked us, like, fifty times. All we did was come in and poke around where we didn't belong, after all."

"Exactly," Joey added. "You just have to promise us that when we come back and visit, we get a discount on the tour of the tunnels."

Monique laughed at that one. "I think I'll be able to manage that."

Jen hugged Monique tightly, saying, "Let's definitely not let so much time pass until the next time we see each other, okay?" Monique agreed, nodding happily as she hugged each of Jen's friends good-bye.

Just before everyone piled into the car, Joey tugged gently on Dawson's sleeve. She had her sketchbook and charcoal in her hand. When they had first set out for New Orleans, Joey thought that she'd spend most of her time drawing. Obviously, other things had gotten in the way.

"Hey Dawson, do you mind if we prolong departure just a minute or two? There's something I kinda wanna do," Joey said quietly.

"Of course," Dawson said. "To tell you the truth, I've gotten pretty fond of this place. What do you wanna do?"

Joey tilted her head, motioning for Dawson to follow her. As their friends were busy loading the rest of their stuff into the car, Joey and Dawson crept around the side of the house.

They arrived at a small, sweet flowering rosebush behind the house. The area looked unkempt, but the bush itself contained some of the most perfect looking roses either of them had ever seen. Joey looked up at Dawson.

"I found it yesterday. Everything seemed so muddled and impossible . . . this is far from the crypt, but it's some sort of memorial. Someone must have believed in her, must have loved her memory as much as Monique. I just wanted to . . ."

Joey trailed off, not needing to explain to her oldest and closest friend what she had to do. She tore out a page from her sketchbook and kneeled down on the moist grass, the roses grazing her dark hair. She brushed some weeds aside to reveal a burnished plaque embedded in the ground. Dawson knelt beside her to read:

> *For Isabella*
> *Who will always be here*
> *Who will always be in love*
> *Who will always be remembered*

Joey peered at Dawson. "Pretty beautiful, huh?"
Dawson nodded. "Pretty beautiful, indeed. I wonder when it's from, who did it . . ."

"I'd like to think it's . . . well, I guess I'd like to think all sorts of impossible things about how this got here. We could say it was a family member, or we could say . . ." Joey trailed off.

Dawson smiled at his friend. "Or we could say that some things are fate."

Joey looked at Dawson for a long moment as the roses stirred gently above them. "You got me," she smiled slowly. "Some things are just fate." Joey, ever good-natured, extended her hand. "So what say we call it a truce?" she asked, rising.

Dawson laughed out loud. "Joey, whatever fake war was going on between us regarding the high falutin' nature of love vanished long ago . . . somewhere in the third tunnel."

"You were keeping track of tunnels? They all kinda melted together for me." Joey smiled. "I guess all I meant was . . . there are some things I fight you on because you're wrong. And believe me, Dawson, you are indeed wrong sometimes. But there are some things I fight you on because, for whatever reason, they scare me. And I can't fight you on fate."

Joey knelt down again, placing her paper on top of the plaque and rubbing her charcoal over it, creating a perfect rubbing of the inscription. She stood up again and walked away with Dawson back to the car in satisfied silence. Something in Joey was finally at peace.

Joey was riding shotgun for the first leg of the trip while Dawson drove. The gang was fairly silent as they pulled out of the driveway and started rolling down the winding road that led away from the Percy

Plantation. They had all experienced so much together that there was nothing for them to do now but reflect on those experiences in silence, and be grateful for each other's company. After all, they had survived a death-defying situation or three.

Jen turned back and gazed at the mansion, the playground of her childhood and the nightmare of her past week. As the sky started to slowly melt from pitch black to a soft, deep blue, the Percy Plantation seemed to ease into a new day. The weariness and gloom that had coated it upon their arrival seemed to be slipping away with the stars. Jen smiled, thinking of the promise Monique now had before her. She found that she couldn't wait to return, which was definitely not what she was thinking two days ago when Pacey was seeing boxes brimming with blood and Jack and Andie were being chased through abandoned warehouses.

Jen looked over at Jack, who was just about to start dozing. She reached over and nudged him. "Hey, Jackers," she said. "New Orleans isn't so scary after all, huh?"

Jack smiled at her, sleepily rolling his eyes. "Just because we made it out alive doesn't mean that everything I originally thought wasn't true. Well . . . maybe with a few adjustments here and there, but still . . ."

He trailed off, nearly dozing, which gave the friends a chance to fall into a brief silence. Every time one of these quiet moments passed between them since the events of the past week, not a single person in that car could keep from replaying in their minds some of the fantastic images they had seen. Their vacation from quiet Capeside had certainly turned into a mystery, and despite the apparent explanations, none of them assumed they would ever really have the answer. Some things, like the way stars connect in the sky like magic, were beyond them. Despite everything they had seen, very little about this world made sense to them. And they assumed it was meant to be that way.

The car hummed over the open road and Dawson picked up speed on the highway. Joey leaned forward, finding an alternative rock station on the radio and turning up the volume. The six friends settled in for the long haul, laughing with each other, beginning to unfold the events that had come to pass as the highway home stretched ahead of them.

About the Authors

Anna Fricke works for "Dawson's Creek" and contributes creative content to its online extension, "Dawson's Desktop." A graduate of Swarthmore College, she grew up in Hancock, Maine and Milton, Massachusetts. She now lives in Los Angeles, California.

Barb Siebertz lives in Burbank, California. *Bayou Blues* is her first novel. She has also written for the hit television series "Dawson's Creek."